No Secrets

Kris Donnell

Contents

Chapter 5   1

Chapter 7   7

Chapter 8   14

Chapter 11   22

Chapter 12   26

Chapter 13   32

Chapter 14   40

Chapter 15   46

Chapter 16   50

Chapter 17   54

Chapter 18   60

Chapter 19   65

Chapter 20   69

Chapter 21   74

Chapter 22   81

Chapter 23   85

Chapter 24   91

Chapter 25   95

Chapter 26   98

Chapter 27   102

Chapter 28   108

Chapter 29   112

Chapter 30   116

Chapter 31   120

Chapter 32   124

Chapter 33   127

Chapter 34   130

Chapter 35   134

Chapter 36   140

Chapter 37   145

Chapter 38   152

Chapter 39   157

Chapter 40   162

Chapter 41   169

Chapter 42   175

Chapter 43   181

Chapter 44   187

Chapter 5

Five days passed since Zayn was really kind to me but at school, he was the ugly feeling less monster, he used to be. He bullied me as usual. And today was the worst day of my life. I will live under the same roof, with my bully and when his friends come to visit him. I will get a beating lesson each time.

It was time for school. I got dressed, I wore a white dress a blue jeans jacket and brown boots and I wore matching a bracelets and I always wore the locket mum gave me. I headed to school and Niall waited for me as we walked together, I was building a great friendship between me and Niall. We became really close friends.

When I got there I had art which means, I get to sit next to Zayn. In the same fucking class room, where we breathe the same air. I mentally rolled my eyes.

I went to the class room and sat next to Zayn, all the time he kept poking me and hitting me and kicking my leg until I just exploded! "Zayn, stop being a child and act like you have a life for a couple of seconds!" I screamed in the middle of the class. Mrs. Sally, our art teacher looked really angry and kicked me out of her class.

'Awesome! Just what I needed. But on the bright side, I was away from Zayn.'

In my free time, I was wandering around, when I felt someone's hand, cover my mouth. It was Harry! He brought me into some old staff room. Where Zayn, Louis and Liam were also there. My eyes widen up and then I felt a hand contact with my face, it was Harry's hand. It hurt me so much.

Liam punched my stomach and I felt my body collapse to the floor. Liam was well built, he was really strong. I tried to gather some power and stand up or at least block any punches or kicks but sadly, I failed. I was too weak. I probably couldn't even stand up for one of them. "P-please stop. I-I can't t-take it." I stutter.

"Well Mariam! I guess that I'm not the child anymore." Zayn grinned at me while kicking my stomach. I felt so dizzy and everything was blur. I saw black spots every where and the sounds were fading, all the names they called me, soon disappeared. And I was stuck in a black void.

*

*

I woke up with Niall next to me. I was extremely confused. "N-Niall?" I asked his face lit up and was focused on me. "I am so happy you woke up!" He said coming closer to me. "Niall, where a-am I?" I stuttered. "You are in my room." He said with a smile.

"I am-What? Dad is expecting me to be home like, right now! What time is it?" I asked. "Mmm-It is 04:17 but don't worry! I talked to your dad. He called on your mobile and you were unconscious, so I answered the phone and told him, I am your friend and we are just hanging out for a little." Niall said to me which I kind of felt a little calm. "I am so sorry but I really need to go. And thank you so much for your help." I hugged him And waved goodbye. "Bye!" He replied.

*

I ran home, I saw dad in the room with tears covering his face. "Dad! I am so sorry I really am." I apologize as I went to him and hugged him, tightly. He hugged me back, like his life depended on it. "I thought you hated me and you don't want to see me." He cried. "No dad! Never! I could never ditch you, I love you with all my heart, dad." I said with hot tears running down my face. "I will miss you so much." I mumbled.

I cried to his muscular chest, "I got you this. So you will never forget me!" Dad tried to crack a smile as he handed me a box.

"I will never forget my one and only father." I replied with a weak smile.

I went up to my room and packed my things I had two suitcases I held one with each hand and looked to my room and I will never forget you, mom.

Some hot tears ran down my face. I didn't care to wip them. I walked down and saw Trisha at the front of the door, waiting for me with a warm smile.

'Why can't Zayn just be friendly and loving like his parents?' I thought as walked to their house.

Their house was huge. Trisha called Zayn "Great!" I mumbled. Zayn came down with a huge smrik on his face. "Zayn! Honey, please take Mariam to her room and help her with her suitcases." she ordered.

"No! It is fine! I will take care of this." I told her "Yeah! She can do it on her own." Zayn said "Zayn, shut up and help our guest her room." Trisha scolded him. Zayn showed me my room and as I entered Zayn placed my bags on the floor. He pushed me and I fell. "Oww.. You prick!" and I stood up and I suddenly saw Zayn behind me "What did you just call me?" He whispered to my face, which made me notice how very close we are! And how very inappropriate this is!

"I said You. Are. A. Prick." I said confidently. "Are you deaf?" I sassed. He looked terribly angry, like was about to murder me or something. But then all of a sudden, he anger turned into a really unsatisfying smirk. I didn't know what is he thinking. And that what scared me the most!

"Oh! believe you, me; this confidence that you think you have will get you nowhere but trouble so don't try it again, for your own good!" He threatened me.

I was unpacking until Trisha called us "Kids! Dinner is ready!" I wore a black jeans and and pink T-shirt and pink vans and took my earphones and my phone. I went down and sat on a chair, which was next to Zayn and Trisha. "The food is really great! Mrs.Malik." I complimented her delicious food. "Oh! Thank you dear. And please call me, Trisha." She said with the biggest smile on her face. Zayn gave me a very weird glare, that I didn't get and then went back to eating.

*

*

I went out just to check on my house which I really missed, by the way. I never said that I hated the Malik's but I did say that I hate Zayn Malik. He was unbelievable. He would do anything just to hurt me. He loves to see me in pain. Although I can't lie, he is quite handsome. But still his ugly and selfish personality destroyed everything!

*

I watched some movies, a lot of movies to be honest. I looked at the clock "Oh my! I have been watching movies for six hours!" I jumped up, turned off the T.V and locked the door. As I was getting out I saw Harry, Liam and Louis at Zayn's house. All of them where sitting in the garden. I turned around but Zayn saw me. "My favorite girl, Mariam." Zayn smirked devilishly at me.

'Fuck you.' I groan, mentally.

'I'm dead. I'm dead. I'm dead. I'm so dead.' I said in my mind.

I take a deep breath and turn around to face these idots. And I decided to put 'Sass' mode on.

"What's up ass-face?" I sassed at him. I am most definitely dead! Zayn rushed up from his seat with his face boiling with anger. "What did you say?" Zayn asked me, as he gave me a chance to take back what I said.

'Please, don't beat me to death!' I begged in my mind.

"You better be fucking high either on your period!" Zayn hissed at me. "Well I am not high! And I am not on my p- What I mean is, I'm not afraid of you." I smirked.

The guys were pretty shocked but Harry, he was smirking and Zayn's face was tomato red. "Cat ate your tongue?" I grin. Zayn was about to slap me but I actually blocked his hand! I couldn't believe what the fuck have I done!

But that feeling didn't last long until Harry slowly, stood up from his chair and walked over to me.

He kicked my leg. "You never ever sass with us bitch! Don't you ever forget who you are! We are the most popular guys in the whole high school and you are just a nobody. We could kill you and we will still be better than you." Harry spat as he moved away only for me to be greeted by a punch from Zayn.

I fell to the floor. Liam picked me up and pined me to the wall "Don't you ever try to sass with us again, do you understand?" Liam hissed at me. I nodded Liam pushed me to the wall harder, that it made my body bounce off the wall."I need an answer!" He said as he punched my gut. "Yes." I spit in his face with all the power left in me.

He let go of me, to wip away my saliva from his face. I took this chance and I ran back to my house and rushed to my bathroom. I looked in my mirror and I saw I had a huge bruise on my jaw line, because of that prick, Zayn. I cried to myself.

I applied some foundation to my face and then I decided to stay in my house for the night. Zayn's stupid friends were still there for what seemed forever. I won't go back to this hell-hole.

I was making a sandwich when my phone started ringing, I looked at Caller ID but it was unknown. I picked up anyways. "Hello?" I said polity "Hey babe! Missed me much?" The guy from the other side said to me.

'I-Is it him-m?' I ask myself, shaking. 'No! It can't be! Can it?'

"Excuse me! Who is calling?" I ask shaking. "Oh My God, babe! Don't tell me you forgot me that fast!" He said in his Spanish accent "Look! I told you to stay away from me! I never want to you again!" I barked to the phone. "But baby, you know I lov-" I ended the phone call. "No! He can't be here!" I say as tear form in my eyes. And then there was a knock on my door.

My body was shaking and heart was aching, soon I wasn't really breathing. Until I opened the door...

....

Please vote and comment

Thanks

Chapter 7

"Who-o's ther-re?" I stutter. No one answered. So I came close then I saw two piercing eyes staring at me.

'Oh my god, please help!', Was all I could think.

I walked closer and the piercing eyes disappeared and a black cat appeared from behind the bushes. "Oh! It was a cat!" I sigh in relief placing a hand on my chest. I turned around and I was about to head towards my house when suddenly, I saw him.

"Missed me?" He said, staring at my lips. Then he started kissing me and I backed away and slapped him. I walked even further from him. Until my back hit my cold house's wall. "M-Mark! Stay away-y f-from me-e!" I stuttered.

"I will take you back, weather you like it or not." He said with a devilfish smirked drawn on his face. I was a little bit scared I got my knife out of my pocket but he saw it and his smirked grew. He pinned to me the wall.

"You know good girls like you shouldn't use this." He said as he kicked my hand and the knife fell from my hand. My eyes widened open. I was about to scream when he stopped me by putting his hand on my mouth. "And also good girls like you shouldn't be up late, all alone, in the streets." He hissed at me as he threw the first punch to my stomach.

"Owe..Mark-k please s-stop.." A few tears run down my face.

His punch was so strong. It hurted more than any hit dad or the boys ever hit me. I have never been in so much pain in my life. "And babe, don't you try to scream for help. Understand?" He snapped at me as he threw the second punch.

I tried to hit him but I failed. "Shouldn't have done that." He grinned. He kneed me in my stomach. "P-please..." I gasp for air, "S-stop-p.." I wasn't able to breathe. He threw uncountable number of punches to my already weak and abused body. "Get-t a-away from me-e!" I tried to make proper words as I tried to push him away. "Don't you ever learn!" He snapped angrily. He grasped on my neck. He was chocking me! I tried to remove his hand but I couldn't. "L-let go-o." I tried to say. He never stopped and my body was getting weaker each second, and the light was getting darker, it was very hard to keep my eyes open anymore. Everything went pitch black.

Zayn's POV:

The last thing I saw was, Mariam making popcorn, I guess. After that I walked to my room and sat in my bed for sometime, until finally, I fell asleep.

*

While I was still in my deep sleep, I heard a huge noise. I walked over to my window. I saw a girl and a guy? I wasn't sure though.

'Eww... Couples!'

'And is this is Mariam? What the actual fuck?!"

I rolled my eyes mentally and when I was going to bed again I saw that the guy wasn't making love to her. He was beating her!

I rushed down and raced to there. I kept looking for them. Until I heard Mariam calling for help "L-let go-o." I heard her again. And I ran towards the sound and saw that guy, he was choking her.

I ran over that guy. "She said let go!" I scream at him. He let's go of Mariam's lifeless body. And she doesn't move an inch. "Oh! And you are Mariam's boyfriend?" He asked smirking.

"First, this is non of your business. And how do you know her name?" I ask him. "Well I guess she didn't tell her little boyfriend about me. I feel really heartbroken." He says with his stupid smirk was growing.

That's when I raced towards him and punched him. He looked away and then he turned back to me. Then he grabbed my shirt's collar "Well listen here, big guy. I am your and her's worst nightmare! And don't try to protect your little princess from me; guess what? You fucking can't." He spit in my face and punched my jaw.

I spit blood from my mouth because of that asshole. I started punching him back but little did he know he will never be able to beat me up. I have been playing boxing for almost three years now.

I kept punching and kicking him, till he fell motionlessly, on the ground. I rushed over to Mariam's aid. I lifted her up. And since I didn't have the keys to her house, I had to take her home. I placed her gently on my bed. She opened her eyes. "Z-Zayn?" She whispered. "Hushh." I shush her. "Zayn, my stomach hurts." She whimpers.

Mariam's POV:

"Zayn, my stomach hurts." I whimper. He lifted my black top. I didn't bother to stop him. He gasped and I couldn't help but cry. "S-stop! Don't cry." He tried to calm me down. "I'm wanna go home." I say trying to stand up. "What? No!" Zayn scolded me. "You are hurt and weak. You probably can't even stand up." He stated. "Not true." I whine. "Look! I'm not gonna argue with you about that. I'm not letting you leave." He told me. "Well, you are not my father, brother or boyfrie-" I was interrupted. "Since you brought it up, who is this guy?" Zayn asked making my heart skip a beat.

"He's a nobody. And he was trying to rob my house but I saw him and tried to stop him. So he saw me and-" I was interrupted again. "Yeah! Good story but do you think I'm stupid?" Zayn asked and before I can answer. "He knew your name!? And he thought I was your boyfriend!" Zayn explains.

"I don't care what you say, I'm going to my house." I stated and he didn't show any emotions.

So I pulled myself up and sat on his bed "Owwe...." I wince in pain. "Here! let me help you." He offered, I nodded defeated as he walked to the bathroom and a couple of seconds he came back. Zayn sat in front of me. Slowly, he raised my top showing my blueish black stomach. He started cleaning my wounds and cuts.

I was biting my lips, to stop myself from screaming. I didn't dare to look at him. "Does it hurt that much?" He asked me. "You are not the one with bruised body, therefore you don't have an opinion." I sassed. "Wow!" He said in amazement. "What?" I hissed. "It's just that you always sass with me in the worst times, I mean you just got a beating, if I just pressed lightly on your stomach. You will die." He smirked at me. I rolled my eyes. "Done!" He announced. I tried to stand up when suddenly I felt everything around me is turing and I felt Zayn's toned muscular arms wrapped around me, protectively.

"T-thank y-you-u.." I stutter. He places me on his bed again. "I don't want 'thank you's, I want an explanation." Zayn gestured for me to spill the beans. "Not gonna happen, Zayn!" I whisper/yell. "C'mon Mary..Please tell me." Zayn whimpered. "No! So back off." I tell him. And he shuts up, finally. Until, he talked again. "Oh C'mon Mariam please tel-" I interrupted Zayn. "Fine Zayn. His name is Mark and he is my ex boyfriend." I told Zayn.

But I wasn't being completely honest with Zayn. Mark and I go way back. Actually Mark's father was a friend of my father. So our dads where really into 'us' being a couple. And I didn't mind it, 'cause Mark wasn't always the cruel, abusive guy he is, now. He was kind, caring and loving. Until his older sister died, he turned into a abuse machine. He would fight about for anything and everything, even if I had nothing to do with it. And when I woke up, dad told me he found a job here, so moved. And I never saw Mark again. Actually I never got time to say my good bye's to him nor break up with him.

"Okay.." He hestitaed. I guess he knows I'm still hiding some secrets. "Anyways, do you have your bedroom keys?" Zayn shot at me. "No I-I forgot t-them." I take some time to answer. "How will you get them? You can't walk home now!" Zayn stated angrily. Then his anger turned into an evil smirk.

"You can join me on the bed if you want?" He smirked. "Never, Malik!" I almost scream. "Well either me or the floor. So choose." He stated with a huge grin on his handsome face. "Okay..." I say in defeat. I walk over his bed and lay down, slowly next to him. "I can't believe I am fucking sleeping next to Zayn Malik.

* The next moring *

I opened my hazel eyes to meet his caramel ones. He was staring into my eyes and I left like he knows everything about me, like he can see everything I am hiding behind them and no matter what I do, or how I try to hide it, he will find it.

While I was deep in thought Zayn moved his face quickly towards mine, causing our lips to crash. He kissed me softly and shockingly, I kissed back. His kiss was too resistible. Our lips moved in sync as if we have kissed before. Sadly, we break our kiss, in desperate need of air. I snapped back to reality.

"Good morning." He grinned yawning. "Morning." I mumbled. "Bye!" I say standing up. "Whoa! Slow down. How are you feeling now?" Zayn asked in a caring tone. "I'm better." I tell him slowing down because of the pain the suddenly occurred in my stomach. "I'll walk you to your house. It ain't far." Zayn says getting up from bed. "No, thank you." I declined his offer. "I said 'I'll walk you to your house.' I don't understand how you heard that as an offer somehow." Zayn mocked. "Whatever, Malik." I groan rolling my eyes.

"Here take this!" Zayn says throwing at me a jacket. "I don't need your help." I stomped my feet like a five year old. "It's 4:00 in the morning. You're gonna freeze if you walk out of the house like this." He groans. "And since when do you care?" I smirk.

Two can play this game. You know.

Zayn's white face blushed in pink. "No, I don't at all." He says trying hide his pink cheeks. I put on his stupid black adidas jacket. It had his cologne. I think I could live here, inside his jacket.

We finally got home. And I kept teasing him all the way home. And so.. did..he back at me. But I actually enjoyed it. I mean he wasn't humiliating me. We were just talking. But the one thing that was stuck on my mind, was the kiss we shared. I kept thinking about it.

"Bye!" He said slaping my arm playfully. "Bye!" I waved back at him. Why does he suddenly seem so attractive to me..

Oh god, I can't be falling for the school's bad boy.

I unlocked the door, to be greeted by warm air hitting sore skin. I took off Zayn's Jacket and placed it softly on the kitchen's island. I walked to my bathroom and looked at my bruised stomach and I applied cream on it.

I have two more hours of sleep before school starts so I better go to bed now. I walked to my bed. The sheets were cold, not like Zayn's warm bed. Zayn's house had a feeling when you go there, you feel like you're happy.

I mean when I first got there I felt loved by Zayn's parents. I felt like I had a family, for first time in a long while. I shifted uncomfortably on bed only to met my mom. I had a framed picture of her next to my bed. "I miss you." I cooed as tear fell from my eyes. Will you ever come back?" I ask the beautiful picture of mom, hoping it would answer me back.

....

Please comment and vote

Thanks

Chapter 8

Daya's song bommed through the air of my quite room. I groaned as I turned off my alarm. I wasn't able to sleep all, I kept thinking about was that stupid kiss.

'Ugh! Why is it bothering me so much? I mean Zayn didn't seem bothered by it at all. He lent me his jacket and walked me home, like nothing happened. Maybe because nothing actually happened..'

I don't know why is it even in my mind. Zayn doesn't care about it so neither do I, Or he does care but he doesn't want to show me...

'Hmpf.. This is enough!' I scream mentally as I walked over to my bathroom, I did my daily routine and walked out, heading to the kitchen. And as I walked down my stomach hurt a little. I am really not a breakfast kinda gal; I can go the whole day without breakfast but dinner is very important to me.

I made myself a caramel latte, I put in it three pink marshmallows. And I sat down to drink it. When my mobile started vibrating. "Hello?" I answered "Hi Girlfriend. How ar-" I cut the caller. "Look Mark I'm not getting back with-" I was interrupted. "Whoa. Slow down girl, it's me, Niall.." Niall explained. "Oh-hi Niall." I say embarrassed. "I'm coming over." He tells me in his Irish accent. "Sure!" I scream like a two year old and hang up.

'I can't believe I didn't fucking look at the caller's ID and save myself the embarrassment.' I groan.

I go up to my room and get dressed into a white crop top and red sweats with white and black converse. I pull my brown hair into a ponytail. I put on some mascara, lip gloss and a little bit of red blush and hell a lot of foundation on my bruised neck and any other visible bruise on my body.

I walked down, jumped on the white couch in the living room and waited for Niall to arrive.

Zayn's POV:

I wasn't really able to sleep well. Mariam fucking kissed me back!? I cannot believe what I am saying. I mean I shared a perfect kiss with someone I never thought I will ever even like!

Anyways, I really wanted to meet her so maybe I could make up an excuse. I put on my black ripped jeans and a white T-shirt with 'Cool Kids Don't Dance' written on it with black. I put on my leather black jacket.

I can't lie, but I was excited to see her. I walked out of my house, made sure the door is locked and walked to Mariam's but then I saw Niall going in.

'Of course! She is in love with him 'cause he is the one who fucking stood up for her first. Bullshit.'

I turn back home, devastated. I can't believe it. Maybe she fucking planned all of this to get back at me. Well not so fast I'll show her who's boss. I grin evily at the thoughts that I have stored for Mariam.

Mariam's POV:

I was wandering through instagram when there was a knock on the door. "Come in, it's open!" I shout. Niall popped out of the door. "Hi!" I scream jumping at him and hugging him. He hugged me back. "I missed you, Bestie." He says patting my head. I smile at him a fake smile. "Niall, I'm not a 2 year old. I tell him sarcastically. "Well but you did sound like one on the phone so I tearted you like one." He replied smiling like an idiot.

"Haha. Very funny Nialler." I pronounce his name in a way different way, which I know he doesn't like, as I grin like stupid. "I hate you." He says walking over to my kitchen and opening the fridge. "Oh please.." I laugh. "Whaf?" He asks with a mouth full of chocolate. "Nothing." I smile.

"You know we need to go to school!" I tell him. Niall huffs, "Fine but let me eat some more chocolate." He said taking more five bars out of the fridge. "Okay Niall, you can take whatever you want, just hurry 'cause we are gonna be late." I shout. "Gee, Okay. Calm down, Mom." He said eating more chocolate and I rolled my eyes.

*

"Bye Niall!" I waved at him. 'Ugh!!' I have History with one and only, Liam Payne. I walk to the very back of the class. And sit there playing color switch on my mobile. When someone walked in. He doesn't look familiar. "Hey.." He said. "Hi." I smile back at him. "Can I sit here?" He asked politely pointing to the seat next to me. "Yeah! Sure." I tell him. "I'm Ryan." He smiled. He was gorgeous. He had blue sparking eyes and blond hair. "Wow!" I mouthed. "What?" He asked. "I'm Mariam." I reply as fast as I can. "There is this question I don't understand, can you help me?" He asks. "Okay." I smile as I start to help him.

Liam walked in and shot me a dirty look. "What's with him?" Ryan asked. "Well we used to be friends but we had a huge fight so we don't talk and we don't like each other anymore." I lie. "Is he your ex-boyfriend?"

"What? No. Never!"

Then I noticed how Ryan looks like a Greek god. He was so hot but not as hot as Zayn.

'What the fu-Did I just say Zayn is hotter than Ryan! And why the fuck do their names rhyme? I still like Zayn's more. I need to fucking shut up.' I scream at myself internally.

"Hey Mariam.. Do you wanna hangout later?" Ryan called. "Yeah, Sure Zayn-I'm sorry I meant Ryan. So sorry Zayn. I mean Ryan." I stutter.

"I need to go now." I say standing up. I walked over to the teacher to ask for permission to go to the restroom and as soon as she agreed I rushed out of the classroom. I went in the restroom, I entered. And locked myself in one of the toilets.

I need to take a deep breath and calm down. I called Ryan, Zayn!? What's wrong with me?

I heard voices. "Hey girl!" One said. "Hey Velma!" The other squeaked also. "Dana, Have you heard about that new guy, his name is Ryan, I guess."Velma said. "He is hot as fuck!" Dana screamed. I rolled my eyes. I try to run away from him and this. "A lot of people say he looks like Zayn." Dana told Velma. "I know, right? But he is like 10x hotter." Velma replies. "No! Zayn is so much hotter. I wish he fucks me." Dana moans. "Slut." I cough and walk out of the toilet Dana shot me a disgusting look while Velma looked deeply embarrassed. "Hi girls." I smirked. "Hey-y." Velma stuttered. "Hello." Dana spat with venom lacing her fake tone. "So I heard that you think that Ryan guy is hot." I say "Yeah! Don't you think so t-" Velma was cut off by Dana. "No not really." She smirked.

"But Zayn is much hotter." She grinned. I don't know why but when she said this. I felt like I wanted to choke her to death. So I decided to play the same dirty game she is playing. "Don't get me wrong but Zayn isn't really a good kisser." I lie. Zayn was the best kiss I ever had. "As for Ryan, well he is polite and he asked me out, oh I'll be sure to tell you if he is a better kisser or not, bye now have a history period with Ryan, I don't wanna keep him waiting." I sass walking out as look back to see Velma hurt and Dana is giving me a death glare. I smirk and turn away.

I was walking in the corridor like a boss 'cause what I did inside there. Oh my god this feeling felt so good, but it didn't last long. When I was about to get in the class, I was pulled from my arm into an empty staff room. 'Uh oh' I thought.

I was about to scream but a hand was placed on my mouth and blocked my mouth. "Hush!" Was what I heard, then the hand was removed slowly. "Z-Zayn?" I ask confused. I saw that no one was with him. Will he beat me? Maybe he'll kiss me or worst, rape me? More thoughts kept floating to my head. "How are you feeling?" He asked with a caring tone.

And I could think was, What. The. Fuck!?

"I'm b-better.." I stutter.

"Really?" He asks worried.

"Zayn, did you hit your head?" I actually ask him.

"What? No. Why?" He asked confused.

I gave him 'What the fuck!?' Look. "You know what, never mind, bye!" I say quickly trying to get out of his grip but I failed. Zayn pulled me back. "Oww.." I mumbled in pain. "Sorry.." He apologizes loosening his grip but he still doesn't let go. I couldn't believe he apologized to me.

Zayn's POV:

I can't fucking believe I apologized to her. What the fuck is wrong with me? This isn't part of the plan. "When you go home, go out of the back gate!" I tell her acting worried. "Wait, why?" She asks. "The boys will be waiting for you at the front gate." I explain.

And let's just say that anything I say is a lie. "And why do you want to help me?" She asks giving the 'do I look stupid' look. She is a smart ass, which kind of makes her so attractive. "I just don't want to carry your useless body all the way home." I rolled my eyes.

She rolls her eyes at me. The amount of sass that girl possesses. I let go of her arm.

Mariam's POV:

Did Zayn just help me?!

He lets go of me arm. I felt butterflies in my stomach. I don't know if it's a good thing or not, it did hurt a little. "Owe." I say as place my hand on it; hoping the pain would stop. "Are you okay?" Zayn shouts. "Yeah, just a little pain." I say trying to stand still. "Mariam, you're bleeding." Zayn tells me. "What?" I ask in disbelief. I slowly slid down until I was sitting on the floor. "Wait, I'll look for tissues." Zayn told me looking around well at least we were in the janitor's closet.

* After sometime *

Of course, the History lesson has ended and I am most definitely never going to the restroom in history class ever again.

I ran to the classroom, I grabbed my stuff and walked out but it's not like I understand anything, anyways.

*

School finished and I was free again. So I headed to the back gate as Zayn told me and while I was walking I heard someone call me "Mariam!" I turned around and saw Zayn. "Yeah?" I answer him. "If you want I can walk you-" Zayn was interrupted by Ryan "Hey Mariam!" Ryan called.

Zayn's POV:

I wanted to walk Mariam home and sneak her to the front gate 'cause I lied. They boys know she goes home from the back gate. And after she touched my hand in the janitor's room, I definitely felt a spark.

I was asking her to walk her home, when a blondie walked towards us. "Hey Mariam!" He ran towards us. "Oh-Hi Ryan." She says. "Do you want a lift home?" He asks her winking. 'What the fuck!'. "Sorry Ryan, I'm taking her home." I say. "Actually-" Mariam was about to speak then I held her hands, she was shocked by my action, and to be honest, I was pretty shocked too but I really wanted to get blondie, here to stay away from Mariam.

"Oh and you are her boyfriend?" Ryan asks looking at her. Before she can a word. "Yes, I am." I say-wait let me correct that, I lie*. Mariam was giving me the 'WHAT?' look. "I don't-you didn't say anything!?" Ryan stutters. "Well she didn't say because the whole school already knows we are the it couple. We are the hottest couple." I roll my eyes.

"Isn't that right, babe?" I pull her waist close to me. "N-Yess..." She plays off. She is the worst actor. I sigh.

Mariam's POV:

I can't believe what is Zayn doing. And I had to lie to Ryan because I don't want a beating. "Bye, Ryan." Zayn smirks evily. Then I pull away from him. "What's wrong with you? Why did you do that?" I ask angrily. "Whoa, slow down there, you are asking to many questions." He says trying to get out of that.

"Zayn, I'm not fucking kidding why did you do that?" I gritted through, my teeth. "You are an asshole, Malik." I say punching his chest, but he didn't even move. "You know what, I'm not even gonna speak to you." I say walking towards the back door.

Zayn's POV:

I can't let her do that! She'll get hurt. So I ran towards her and grabbed her arm. She turned her face to me. She was staring at me angrily. I didn't know what to do or what to say?

I did the first thing that popped to my mind, so I kissed her. I cupped her cheeks and kissed her passionately. And soon enough, I wasn't doing it to distract her, I was doing it because I like her. I can't lie to myself anymore. And the strangest thing is she kissed back. I love her soft pink lips. I pull her waist closer. She moves her fingers through my hair.

Then we pulled back her face was tomato red, just like the first time we kissed.

....

Hope like this chapter. This one is 2428 words.

Please vote and comment

Thanks

Chapter 11

"So what do you wanna watch?" Zayn asks me heading over to the DVD player. "Nerve." I say smiling like stupid. "This movie is quite boring. I like something more like Deadpool." Zayn grinned. "Whatever." I rolled my eyes.

"Fine, here is your boring movie." Zayn sighed placing in Nerve. "That's more like it." I smirk. Oh My God! I am in love with Dave Franco. "That dude is very stupid." Zayn shouts. "No, he is not. He is kind and loving." I defend Dave. "Yeah! Sure." Zayn rolled his eyes. "I think he is very hot, actually I would love have a little fun with him." I smirk. "But yesterday you seemed so pleased with me." He grinned devilishly. My face turned to the a dark shade of red.

Zayn's grin grows even wider than before as he slides closer to me and I take a step away, but he moves closer again and as I try to move away, I end up falling on my bum. "Owe. That hurts." I fake cry. "You deserve it; cause you were trying to get away from me." He smirks, helping me up. "Ha. Ha. Ha." I laugh sarcastically. "I love it when you talk dirty to me." I roll my eyes. He smirks and comes closers. "I know, babe." He whispers in my ear, then he kissed my cheek, making my whole face turn tomato red.

"C'mon, we are gonna be late for school." I tell him, making him groan. "We were having a good time. Why do you have to be such a mood killer?" Zayn pouted. I snickered as I walked up to Zayn's room; to get dressed. 'Cause you know I will here for a lot of time, and Zayn's parents are not here, so Zayn suggested I move in with him; in his own room, so he could take care of me. But he was the one who offered me to stay.

I really don't know what's the relationship between us is called. I mean; we are not 'friends with benefits' as people say, we are more like 'enemies with benefits'.

I walked in Zayn's room, looking for anything mine, so I could wear it. While I was wandering around I saw a dress, that I haven't wore in a lot of time, not since I stopped dating Mark; cause he got it for me. I froze in my place.

'No, I can't. It brings too many unpleasant memories.' I tear spilled from my eye. I grabbed it, throwing it in my bag. Then threw on a white sweater and black skinny jeans. I let my hair down. And walked down, to Zayn. "Done." I announce hopping in the room. "I'll go get dressed then we could go to school." He tells me and I nod in return.

Zayn and I were walking to school "So see ya later." I wave at Zayn. "Later." He waved back. I walked to my first class English with Niall. Soon enough the school day was almost over, still one lesson to go. I walked over there 'cause I don't wanna be late. I had chemistry and the teacher kept going on and on and on, like it was never gonna end. Two fucking hours left! I will never be able to survive. I sunck out slowly.

'Yes, finally ditched fucking school. Fuck you, chemistry!'

I felt victory and happiness run through my blood. I skipped happily in the streets until I was in front of a lake. I stopped there and got the dress out my bag, I started at it and studied it carefully. "Screw you too." I scream throwing it in the lake.

Finally, I'm sure I'll never see that dress again. I was about to walk away but a hand was placed on my mouth blocking my screams.

Then I smelled a funny oder, making my body weaken and light turn into darkness. I felt so weak and powerless. The other person that I couldn't see, was pulling me, far away from the lake.

Suddenly, I felt that person turn me to face him but before I could see his face, a strong punch was sent to my face making me black out completely.

*

I was on the cold ground, in a dark place where seemed like the light has never met. I tried to move, but I noticed I was tied. I was so scared, I don't know what to do.

'Where am I anyway?' I wonder.

I kept squirming around, hoping that I might get out. It was no use, I was tied very hard that nothing happened but my hand got bruised.

Out of the blue, while I was very busy, trying to escape, the door opened. It revealed a huge silhouette of male, that I couldn't see again 'cause the light was in my eyes. The person walked towards me, while my whole body was shaking badly. Then he was so close that I could feel is breaths on my neck. "W-who are you-u?" I stutter. I felt him smirk. "I'm your worst nightmare." He whipstered in a deadly tone, making all the air in my lungs disappear.

"It can't be." I cry. "You had your chance and you fucking blew it." He spat at me. I flinched as he said these words with venom filled his mouth. I tried to take a deep breath, but I want even able to think straight. "Please don't hurt me." I sob hopelessly. "Sorry, I think this is why I brought you here."

He grins as he finally showed his face. I was pretty shocked. But all I could think about was how this is gonna hurt like hell.

....

Heyy! Happy Valentine's day

So sorry the chapter is short but I have no idea, what to do?

Please vote and comment

Thanks

Chapter 12

Zayn's POV:

School just finished, so I went out to look for Mariam, but she wasn't at her class. I saw Niall, he was standing looking like he was waiting for someone, Mariam, I bet. I should ask him if he saw her. "Hey Niall!" I shout grabbing Niall's attention. "Hey." He replies. "Have you seen Mariam?" He asks me. "No, actually I was about to ask you the same." I tell him. "I had English with her earlier." He says. "I'll call her." I take out my mobile and search for her contact. Then Mariam's voicemail started speaking. I closed the phone angrily. "She is not answering." I state pissed off. "We need to look for her." Niall announces and I nod in return.

*

Niall and I have been looking for Mariam, everywhere. We also tried calling her, but it's no use. I was searching for her next to the highschool, but there was no sigh of her anywhere. It's like she disappeared into thin air, or like the ground swallowed her up. My heart was about to stop when I thought Mark may have hurt her, or maybe he kidnapped her. Niall was at the my house, in case she comes home.

I dialed Niall's phone number, he picked up. "Any sign of her?" I ask. "Nope." He said popping the 'p'. I could sense disappointment in his voice. "What about you?" He asked me. "Nothing at all. I don't understand, how could she disappear like this?" I mutter. "I'll keep looking, I gotta go." I inform Niall and hang up. Then I saw Louis and Liam taking. Thus I eavesdropped. "Hey lad! Have you seen Harry?" Louis asks Liam. "No. I haven't seen him all day." Liam tells Louis.

"Wanna go at my place?"

"Sure." Liam nods and they both walk away.

This is definitely not good. Harry and Mariam are missing. I don't know if there is connection between both of their disappearing. I want to know more about Harry's disappearing, but still Harry might have just ditched school.

Mariam's POV:

"Shut up bitch!" He screamed at me as he was kicking me. "P-please stop-p." I cry running out breath. "You are so pathetic and unbelievable." He spat at me. He slapped me, making my body collapse to the floor. I stayed there, I can't dare to look at him or even try to move. "You are the reason my life turned like this! Cause you ruined it, you spoiled brat." He yelled at me as he kicked my leg. "Oww." I screamed in pain. "What did I ever do to you?" I sobbed hoping this torture will end. "You destroyed everything I love, you killed the one and only hope in my miserable life. How are you even able to live like that?" He shouted as he kicked my side a lot of times, that I lost count. Tears raced down my face.

He untied my hands and he grabbed a fist full of my hair. He yanked me up, until I was standing on my feet. Then pinned me to the wall, and threw an uncountable number of punches to already bruised stomach. The punches stopped my lungs from breathing. "I-I can't breathe-e." I mumbled between my weeping. He let's go of my body and I fall despairingly to ground again.

He stepped on my arm, that it made a crack sound. Every thing was turning darker. All the pain in my arm, on my side and in my stomach was fading second by second. Maybe I might die, and all this pain will end. He finally walked away. And slamming the door behind him. New tears threatened to spill out of my already sore and red eyes, but I blinked them away. I curled up into a ball and buried my bruised face in my knees. I can hardly breathe. "Please anyone! Help me.." I mumble through the tears.

Zayn's POV:

I have been looking for Mariam for the whole day. Not a call, not a text, nothing. I can't believe she disappeared like that.

In that moment, I was sure she was in danger. I mean; she wouldn't run away from me, would she? I started questioning everything.

"Mariam, please pick up." I cry at the phone, but it sends me to her voice-mail again. "Bullshit!" I scream into the air. I walked home desperately, hoping she would come.

I changed my clothes and then I sat in front of the door, wishing she would show up. I haven't eaten anything and I don't want to. I really need to find her. 'But how?' I wonder in distress.

Then out of the blue, my mobile buzzed with a message. I read it, it said, I will ruin your life forever and I hope you know your stupid girlfriend is the reason. Sincerely, Mark. I was boiling with anger as soon as I read this Message and this moment I was sure he did something to Mariam.

Mariam's POV:

I was badly hurt. I couldn't sleep, I was afraid he'll hurt me while I am sleeping. I haven't eaten anything all day. I felt like I was dying.

I tried to crawl around to look for anything that could help get out of here. I couldn't move a muscle, but I tried with all my power. As soon as I stood up I felt everything spin around me. I leand on the wall and looked around I saw my phone! It was broken. I ran towards my phone. "Please work." I plead in despair. I breathed heavily as I dialed Zayn's number. I was so worried, he might come in.

Then Zayn picked up! I felt my heart skip a beat. I couldn't believe it, this torture will end. "Mariam?" Zayn asked in disbelief. "Zayn. It's me. Please help me! I am kidnapped." I cry in a low voice. "Who k-kidnapped you-u?" He stutters. "He's-" I was cut off by him walking in. I felt like my heart was in my mouth. My breathing got messed up. "You bitch!" He roared as he kicked my ribs. I just froze there. He yanked me from my hair and threw me to the wall. I could feel a warm liquid running on my forehead, down my cheek. "Who the fuck told you to move?" He yelled irritated.

"I-I am s-sorry. P-please don't beat-t m-me." I managed to say. "I don't think so." He grasped my neck tightly and held me against the wall. "P-please I-I can't b-breathe." I stuttered but he grabbed my neck tighter. I wasn't able to breathe at all. My vision was blurry and I couldn't see anything, I felt so numb. He let go of my wounded neck. I fell to the ground on the floor, gasping for air. I felt so lifeless.

'What did I ever do to him? I never knew anything about him. How could I destroy his life?'

Some tears raced down my face. He kicked my stomach over and over again. He never stopped. "You fucking tried to call Zayn?" He spats with venom lacing his voice. "I-'m sorry," I paused. I wasn't able to talk anymore. I wanted to eat, to sleep and to get out of here. But I couldn't even keep my eyes open, that I passed out.

Zayn's POV:

This is so not satisfying. This call made me even more worried. Mariam's voice was so broken. I must find her. Maybe I could track her mobile. So I woke Niall up, to tell him about what happened. Niall was crashing at mine. "Niall, wake up!" I yell. "What?" He asks worriedly. "Mariam called me." I paused and Niall eyes widen open. "She told me, she has been kidnapped." I break. "By who?" Niall's face was white. "I-I don't-t k-know. She was cut off, I heard him scream at her then the call ended." I explain. "We need to find her now!" He says getting from the couch. "I could track her phone." Niall offered. "Then come on." I say and he nods. "But I hope you know this will take some time." Niall informs me. "I know." I nod accepting.

three days later

Mariam's POV:

This is my fourth day here. I didn't eat or drink anything. I was so weak, that I couldn't move. My mobile was lying at the end of the room, on a high dirty closet, but I wasn't able to move. I could barely open my eyes. I have been getting a daily beating. My whole body was bleeding and my stomach was colored in blue, black and purple.

The door flew open again showing the person I hate the most, him. "Please don't hurt me." I beg him. But he was stone hearted and mercyless. He didn't even respond to me, he just started abusing me again. My head was throbbing badly. He kept kicking me, until I was in a lot of pain again. I noticed he stopped and he was staring my stomach, which I noticed, that it was bleeding and I was lying in puddel made of my own blood. Everything was getting so dark, till my whole vision turned into pitch black

....

Hey everyone! Happy Valentine's day again. Here two updates in one day

Please vote and comment.

Thanks

Chapter 13

H arry's POV:

Yesterday, after she started bleeding, I decided to stop, maybe this is enough. I walked out slamming the door.

Next day

I got off of my bed. I was analyzing the kitchen's wall. I don't understand, how is she still alive it's been four days and she didn't eat or drink anything. I walked up and got ready to beat Mariam again. I hate her name. Roughly, I pushed the basements's door open, to see her in the corner, she wasn't moving. I walked towards her. "Stand up bitch." I yell. She moves her head slowly. "P-please, d-don't h-hu-rt me-e." She stutters. Her face was covered in blood, all of her body was actually.

"I said get up." I said firmly. She was shaking terribly as she tried to stand up, but failed and she fell back hitting her back to the wall. She was biting her lips as she looked into my eyes. Her stare it reminded me of mom. She had the same pain look in her eyes. I couldn't believe it. "I beg you, please s-stop." She cries her eyes out. I didn't know what to do. I was lost in deep thought. But then I remembered what she did to me.

I kicked her getting all my anger out. "Owe.." She bawls her sore eyes out, but she deserved this. I kicked her body more couple of times until she stopped moving completely.

'This is not good.' I thought.

Zayn's POV:

I have no fucking idea where Mariam is. I couldn't track her stupid phone. She has been lost for four days. I'm dying from inside. Niall never left my side, which made me know, how much of a great friend he is, and how I let him down. I was stupid for doing this and I regret it.

Then there was a knock on the door. My face lit up like a two year old. Could it be? Has she finally came back? I thought happily, but all my dreams crashed when I saw Louis. "What do you want Louis?" I spat with venom. "There is something I must tell you, but before I do, you must calm down." He told me but this made me even angrier. "Louis, if you have anything to say, fucking do it 'cause I don't have time for this shit." I tell him closing the door but he stops me.

"I know where Mariam is." He says quickly. And as soon as I heard these words, my blood boils with anger. "You are so fucking dead, Tomlinson." I yelled as I jumped on him and threw an uncountable number of punches to his face, which was now bleeding because of me. "Zayn! What are you doing?" Niall shouts at me as he gets me off of Louis. "He fucking knows where is Mariam and he never told us." I groan. Niall looked at Louis, "Where is she?" He screams. "S-she's at-t Har-ry's." He stutters. I was filled with fear. I yanked Louis into the backseat of my car and Niall sat next me.

I drove as fast as I can to Harry's house. I dialed his phone number. It was ringing and he actually picked up. "Harry, you son of a bitch, I hope you rot in hell. You mother fuc-" I was cut off by him. " Zayn, Mariam is not breathing, but her heart is still beating." He said worried. "Fucking take her to the nearest hospital, you fucking idiot." I cruse at him and with that he hangs up.

*

Harry texted me the address. I drove to the hospital. And I rushed in looking for Mariam. I rushed to the first nurse I saw. "What room is Mariam Anderson?" I ask her. "She is in room 258." She tells me checking her clipboard. "Thank you." I say racing in the halls trying to find her room, until I did. I walked in, she was laying lifelessly on the white hospital bed. Her face was covered with cuts, bruises, wounds and scratches. A huge air mask was placed on her pale face. I walked over close her motionless body and kneeled down. "Thank god, you're alive." I whisper in her ear. I kissed her forehead, softly.

Then Harry walked in. And I exploded. "You are a feeling-less manwhore." I spit at him, punching his face. He fell back from the impact of the hit. He had a black eye. "You have one second to start explaining yourself or I will murder you, right here, right now." I spat at him. "I will tell you everything." He said defeated.

"I'm-" He was cut off by Niall, Louis and Liam, entering the room. "What is he doing here?" I question, pointing to Liam. "Louis called him." Niall explained. Then I turned back to Harry. "Continue." I ordered him. "I'm her half brother." He says in a low voice. "You are a monster." Niall mumbles. I was so shocked that I wasn't able to speak. "You mean that you have been beating her up for four days, starving her to death and bulling her and she is your sister." Liam reconnects the dots, pretty shocked as well. "Screw you." I roar punching him over and over. "She is dying because of you asshole." I snap at him I didn't realize that my eyes were tearing up. He didn't defend himself nor tried to block any of my hits.

The doctor walked in and I jumped off of Harry. The doctor didn't seem happy. "Hello." She greeted. "Hey." Niall replied. "I need to tell you that

Mariam's condition is very serious and private. I could only tell anyone who's related to her." She informed us and we noddedd. "I'm her hal-" I cut Harry off, "I'm her fiancé." I say out loud to the doctor. All the boys were staring at me, but I didn't care. The doctor nodded towards me, "It's okay, they are my friends." I tell the doctor so she can speak in front of the others. She clears her throat then starts speaking, "Mariam is very sick, she has a broken arm, some torn joints, but worst of all, she has a kidney failure, due to a deep cut in her side, which got infected.

We tried to clean it and it did help a little but you should have brought her earlier." She paused taking deep breath. I was about to pass out. Harry fucking cut her open. "She needs a kidney transplant as soon as possible, 'cause she won't be able to live without it." Dr. Marie breaks the news to me. I felt everything around me is spinning.

After a few seconds, an idea popped in my mind. "I'll give her my kidney!" I say. Dr. Marie stares at me, "Sir, Are you sure?" She asks me, formally. I nod back to assure her. "Fine, but we must see if your kidney matchs her's." She informs me. I nod again. "Okay sir, follow me then." She tells me and I do as told.

Harry's POV:

'What have I done? I almost killed her. How did I turn into such a monster? I bet mom will be deeply disappointed in me.

'I'm sorry, mom. I'm sorry that I failed you, and became everything you raised me not be. I'm sorry that I hurt your one and only daughter. I'm sorry I blamed her for something she never did. Please tell me what to do for you to forgive me.' I cry.

I wish my hand would have fell off before I tried to hurt her like that. I was in great pain when I saw her looking like that. If only I realized that earlier, she wouldn't have been in all of this.

Zayn's POV:

I was done with tests. I hope we match. I had a bad headache, ever since Dr. Marie told us about Mariam. I walked over Mariam's lifeless body, I grabbed a chair and sat next to her. "Mariam, I hope you can hear me. I want you to know that I wasn't messing around like I do with other girls, the day we kissed made me feel something. I-I love you." I whisper to her hair. "I'll do anything for you to wake up. I'm very sorry, this is all my fault if only I saved you earlier, you wouldn't be here. You would have been home, with me and we will be fighting over what movie to watch." I crack a teary smile. I never felt this love towards someone. "Please, you can't leave me now!"

"Please, you gotta wake up." I cry.

*

It's been 8 hours. We are waiting for my results to come out. Then Dr. Marie entered. "I have the results." She announced. I couldn't read her face expression, so I didn't know if it was good news or not. "I am sorry but they don't match." She says in a low voice. "What?" I feel my breathing get messed up. "No! We have to try again. Maybe the results are wrong." I yell. There is no way, I'll let Mariam fall out of my hands. "Please you have to save her." I cry. "We need to find another person that matches her, sir." She tells me. "I will give her mine." Harry states out of the blue. "Then please follow me." She ordered and he followed her and disappeared into the distance.

2 days later

Harry's POV:

Its been two days and Mariam didn't even wake up. and we are all crashing at the hospital, and non of us has the guts leave. We are all so dead worried. Dr. Marie told us that my kidney matches Mariam's, and this is a little bit satisfying, but they can't do the surgery now; Mariam's body is too weak, right now.

I got up from the hospital's couch and walked over to Mariam's bed, I watched her there lying on the bed, so lifeless. This was the only world I could describe her in. I walked towards her and sat on a chair beside her and held her hands, they were so cold. all these machines glued to her. The air mask was still on her face, and her face was still full of cuts, so as all her body and her broken arm she looked like she was hit by a bus. Tears were spiling out of my eyes. "Mariam, I am so sorry. I will make it up to you, just please wake up. I am begging you wake up please, would you?" I cried to her, wishing she could hear me. I felt a hand on my shoulder, it was Niall, he had tears running down his face "Don't worry, mate. We are all beside her." Niall told me. I gave him a weak smile. Then I walked out. I needed some fresh air.

Niall's POV:

As harry walked away "That son of a bitch-!" Zayn screamed as Harry left. "Zayn, don't judge him, you don't know what he has through; he lost his mother, and now he is losing his sister." I screamed at him. "Well, that's because of him, or do you have any other stupid reason?" Zayn screamed back, I kept silent. "Well! That's what I thought too." He yelled. "Guys! Break it up, would you? I think it will be a good idea, if we go out and get some food and I actually really need to check on my sisters." Louis suggested. "No! I am not leaving Mariam, not until she wakes up." Zayn stated. "C'mon Zayn, we will go get food, then we'll come back." Liam told Zayn. "Okay, but we will come back quickly." Zayn demanded. "Okay, mate." Liam replied.

They all walked out. I looked at Mariam, one last look. Then got out everyone went on their own way.

Mariam's POV:

Slowly, I opened my eyes, with my body, hurting me, terribly. All these machins attached to me, hurt me also.

I don't know how did I end up here? The last thing I remember was that I was at Harry's basement. And he was beating me everyday. There is no way he would have help me. "Hey." I said to the nurse who came in. "Oh! My thank god. That you're up, the docter thought that your body was too weak to wake up." she said to me, I stood there quitly until there was a knocking sound on the door. "Come in, boys she's up!" said the nurse smiling then appeared five boys. My eyes widen open, "I have missed you so much." Zayn said as he hugged me, tightly. I hugged him back. "I was so worried about you." Niall said as he held my hand. "Thank you, Niall." I thanked as I gave him a weak smile. Liam just smiled at me, but my smile fell when I saw Louis and Harry. Louis moved forward to me. "Hey em-Mariam-I-I know you probably hate me, and will never forgive me. But I am really sorry." Louis said to me with guilt in his eyes. "Okay Louis." I say with forgiveness. He smilies at me, but Harry just walked away.

After a lot time. All the boys went back home, for just a little bit, Zayn promised he'll come back but he needed to change. Harry, he wanted to stay, he slept with me, in the same room, but on another bed, I was totally confused.

'Why did he do this?'

His eyes were filled with guilt. I slept with a lot of thoughts running in my head.

*

I wake up because of the beeping sounds next to me. I see Harry's bed is empty, then I see someone standing by the window. It Harry! And he was crying !? What the hell is going on? Why is he crying? He is mumbling something.

"Mariam, I am really sorry, I blamed you for something you never did .I am the worst person." I heard him cry.

The nurse entered the room with a metal tray, there were three needles on the metal tray. Harry moved near me. "Miss, you need to take your medicine today." I nodded unsure.

"Emm.... Want me to hold your hand?" Harry asked me, I nodded, not thinking as I was really scared of needles. I needed someone to be next to me. He moved next to me, and then jumped on my bed, and he held my hand, tightly, while the nurse got in the injections in my arm.

He is my bully and he almost killed me. Then I let go of his hug, he looks a little bit broken. "Look Mariam, there is something I must tell y-" Harry was interrupted by Zayn, suddenly, he was holding something behind his back.

....

Hey guys! Hope you like this one

Please vote and comment.

Thanks

Chapter 14

Zayn's POV:

I heard Harry was about to tell Mariam, that he is her brother, but I wasn't about to let that happen. I walked in with some flowers, which I hid behind my back. She smiled in my way. "Hey!" I said breaking up the silence. "H-hey." Mariam stuttered, "Are you okay?" I screamed running towards her aid. "I'm fine." She said out loud. "P-please don't-t leave me alone w-with Harry-y." She whispers in my ear. She was really afraid of him. I gave her the flowers that I got her, she smiled and mumbled me, a thank you.

I walked over to Harry, as if I was greeting him, but actually I was giving him a message. "Don't tell her anything, and if you even think about trying to hurt her, I will beat you to death." I threaten Harry. He glups, nodding.

"Mariam, I am really sorry for what I have done to you, but I swear I was out of my mind, I know there in no way you could forgive me, but could you give me a chance please." Harry begged Mariam. "I-I," She was at loss of words. "I really don't k-know. I can't real-" she wasn't able to form words.

"You can answer me later." He smiled at her, I know Harry's her brother but I feel so jealous. So I place my hand over her waist and pull her closer. She winces, "Ouch." A tear spills from her sore eyes. "Sorry." I apologized. I can't believe how could Harry do this to her?

"I hope you know, that I'm deeply sorr-" Harry apologized again. "Harry, before you apologize again, you should know that what you did to me is unforgivable. You had billions of chances, instead of millions but you never stopped, you always went further and tried to hurt me more. You were starving me to death." Her eyes were glassy. "So I'm gonna need a lot of time, but before anything, I need to know why did you do this?" She asked him, which made my heart ache.

I really didn't want Harry to tell Mariam, I don't wanna know how will she react. She is very sick right now. Harry gave me 'I'm sorry' look and started to spill, "I'm-" Here it comes....

Mariam's POV:

Finally, I'll know why I have been tortured all my life. "I'm-" Harry was cut off by Dr. Marie walking in. "I can see you're doing a lot better," She smiled. "So any pain?" She asks. "Yeah, my side hurts, a lot." I speak truthfully. "Oh, that must be because of the surgery." She smiled assuring me. "W-what s-surgery?" I was very confused. "Miss, did no one tell you? You had a kidney failure, so you friend, there helped you. I should tell you he is a hero. You would have never made it without him." She explained to me, referring to Harry as 'my friend'.

"H-harry? Y-you-u helped me? I mean w-why?" I ask running out words. "I'll leave you alone, now." Dr. Marie said walking out. "Why?" I ask again. "Because, I'm your-r-" Harry was interrupted by Zayn. "Your friend! He's your friend." Zayn said quickly, but I could sence something wrong. "No, Zayn!" Harry groand angrily. "I'm your half brother." He said. "What?!" I literally scream. "Mariam, calm down." Zayn tells me. I try to breathe. "Are you kidding?" I ask. I felt everything was spinning, my heart monitor was making a lot of noises. "Dr. Marie!!" Zayn screamed. Lights and sounds were fading, until a cloud of unconsciousness washed over me.

*

I heard a beeping sound next to me. "W-what happened?" I questioned. All eyes in the room were staring at me. Even Liam, Louis, Niall and Dr. Marie were all here. "Miss Anderson, you fainted and this isn't right. You should rest, and eat, a lot." Dr. Marie warned me. "When can she go home?" Zayn asked. "I'm sorry but I can't answer that question; before she can go home, we must make sure she is healthy again." Dr. Marie took a brief look at my file. "And by this rate, I'm deeply sorry to say, not anytime soon." She stated, Zayn nodded understanding.

He walked over to me. "I promise, you're gonna be okay." He gave me a reassuring smile. I cracked a weak smile. "But did anyone of you know that Harry's my brother?" I mumble. "Well, we did know before you did with a little." Niall answered truthfully.

"So you were going to keep this from me?"

They all looked away. "Not forever, but I was worried you might get all freaked out." Zayn explained. "This isn't a reas-" Before I could finish my sentence, I felt my chest raising up and down. "Just take a deep breath." Liam told me, slowly. I nodded and did as told. "Let's drop this, please." Niall asked, I nodded, gaining control of my breathing.

*

The whole day passed and Dr. Marie said I was getting better and If I was still okay till tomorrow, I will able to go home soon. A nurse walked in with another tray full of injections. 'Just great!' Note the sarcasm.

I took a deep breath and never let it out. I kept trying to get my mind to think of anything else but I failed. The pain was unbearable. I saw Zayn walking next to me, with a warm smile drawn on his face. He held my hand and I grabbed his back. Soon enough, the blooldy nurse was done making holes in me. "Thank you." I mumbled. He kissed my forehead.

'Why did Zayn suddenly change?' I ask.

I really did want to know the reason, but still I loved it. Zayn has became caring, loving and kind. And honestly, I never thought that 'My bully', Zayn Malik had a soft side where he can be the perfect guy.

* The next day *

I got up from bed early. Finally, I changed back into my clothes. Zayn was next to me all the time, he checked me out and he held me hand all the way to his house. Zayn opened the door for us to enter. I did so and walked to his room. I threw myself on the bed and he jumped next to me.

"Hey, it's been so long since we made out." He smirked. "First, there is this question, which is killing me alive," I stop waiting to see his reaction. "Go ahead." He smiles. "Why did you change?- I mean all of a sudden, you care about me and-" He places a finger on my lips, gesturing me to stop blathering on. He licked his bottem lip and then spoke. "I changed because, deep down, I knew what I was doing was wrong, and it needed to stop before it got too serious." He explains running his hand through his jet black hair, which made him sexier that anything you could imagine.

"And I really feel something for you." He spilt the beans. "W-what?" I choke on my slaiva. "As I said, I like you, Mariam Elene Anderson." Zayn yelled my full name. I couldn't take it anymore, I jumped at him and kissed him, wrapping my legs around his waist. He held me and kissed me back passionately. "I don't think you're so bad yourself." I sassed. Our kissing soon turned into a making out session.

*

I was lying next to Zayn on his bed. The T.V was on, making me groan from the noise. I tried to get up, but I noticed that Zayn was gripping on waist. I smiled and truned to face him. He was sleeping, he looked so sexy. I played with his soft hair. He looked like an angle. Then he opened one eye and analyzed my face, then smirked.

Out of the blue, he got up and jumped on me he started kissing me as he slowly moved lower and lower, till he reached my neck and by mistake I moaned his name! He smirked like a devil and he started leaving love bits whenever he could. I bit my lower lip, trying to moan again, only this time will be a lot louder.

He lifted my shirt slowly, and then he gasped in horror. "Z-zayn, i-is there-r something-g w-wrong?" I struggle with words. "Did he do this?" Zayn asked gesturing to my purple blueish stomach. I nodded slowly. Zayn moved closer to my ear. "I'm so sorry, I didn't help you earlier." He apologized. Flashbacks came back from the previous days, making tears spill out of my eyes.

"Babe, are you okay?" Zayn asks. It was the first time he called me 'Babe' but still the memories of the torture, floated in my mind, making tear rush out of my eyes. "I'm so sorry, I didn't mean to-I mean did I hurt you?" Zayn boomed at me. "It's o-okay." I stutter, when I felt two toned muscular arms were wrapped around me protectively. "Shhh, don't cry." He hushed me softly. I hugged him back as he held my fragile body against his muscular chest.

"Thank you, Zayn. Thanks so much for helping me. I really need you by my side right now."

"I always will."

"Really?"

"I promise."

He kissed my forehead, and we hugged till we fell asleep. I really hope Zayn keeps his promise.

....

Please comment and vote

Thanks

Chapter 15

My eyes fluttered open, just to meet Zayn's caramel ones. "Good Morning, babe." He says in his sexy British accent. "Morning." I peeked his lips quickly. "Finally, the weekend." I scream into the void and Zayn laughs. "What do you wanna do today?" He asks me jumping out of bed. "I wanna go out; I'm not gonna sit in any more beds!" I pout like 5 year old. "What? No!" Zayn boomed. "You got out of the hospital yesterday. I was only asking you, 'What do you wanna do?' As in like do wanna go downstairs, and watch a Movie, or something like that?" Zayn explained to me. "I wanna get out of the house." I frown.

"Fine."

"Really?"

"Yes, of course."

"Where will go?" I ask jumping

"We could go to your house-"

"No Malik! I wanna go somewhere, not a house." I shout angrily.

"These are only places we could go to because you still need to rest." He told me.

"Fine!" I stick my tongue at him, he smirks at me. "Go get dressed; I have an idea." He orders me, I nod and obey him. "Get out." I say. "No need, I'm staring to get used to it." He grins. "Get out, you pervert." I yell. He glances at me one last time then walked out.

I stripped all my clothes, and put on my skinny white jeans and my black top. I could have worm my crop top but I have hideous scars and bruises. I slip on my black vans. Then I walked over to the mirror, but what I saw no make up could fix. I had a black eye, my lower lip was cut, my left cheek was purple and my neck was all blue and black. I grabbed my make up and started trying to hide all these ugly bruises.

'How could Zayn live with someone as ugly as me?'

'How could he kiss me, hug me and tell me that I'm beautiful?'

A tear rolled down my cheek at the horrible memories. While I was still analyzing my pale face, the door opened. Zayn rushed in he was wearing a black shirt, blue ripped jeans and a huge puff olive jacket, but he had one shoe on.

"Mariam, have you seen where is my other shoe?" He asked me.

I turned to him and his face turned white. "Are you okay? Is something hurting you?" He asked with worry lacing his voice. "No. I-I just want to know why did you lie to me?" I murmured, before he could speak, I continue, "How could tell me that I'm beautiful, while I'm not?"

Another tear rolled down. He raced towards me and pressed me into his chest. "I never lied, I don't think you're beautiful. I know you're gorgeous. I can see beneath all these beautiful scars," Zayn kissed a huge scar which was on my hand. "I can see a strong girl, who has been through a lot but yet, she is still holding on, she is still smiling and she is giving everything she can." Zayn mumbles into my hair. I grab to him tighter as a teary smile was placed on my face.

Suddenly, my legs weren't on the floor anymore. Zayn was carrying me, then he threw me on the bed. He pulled up my shirt only to show more bruises and wounds. He smiled at me, "As I told you, I can only see beneath all these beautiful scars." Zayn mumbled as he kissed my stomach, softly.

And soon enough, he lifted my shirt even more, it showed more cuts and bruises. Zayn pushed my shirt further and over my head. I was only in my purple bra. He kissed me passionately. "I love every single inch of you." Zayn gazed into my eyes. I felt butterflies in my stomach. "I love you, Zayn." I take a small break from kissing him and then we continue. Our kissing soon turned into a making out session, as always. "Zayn, I really hate to break up this, but if we don't get dressed now, I won't be able to see your idea." I tell him. "That's okay, I like the dark, maybe we could make out little." He whispered. "Haha." I laugh sarcastically.

"Sorry, babe I gotta go finish your surprise." He apologizes with a kiss then gets up and walks towards the door. "Wait here! And don't get out until I tell you!" He points his index finger at me. "Okay, whatever." I pout. "Aww... You look cute when you act like a kid." He mocked peeking my cheek then he ran out of the room. I put my shirt back on.

'What is he gonna do?' I wonder, curiously.

45 minutes later

Curiosity was literally killing me. I tried to play on my phone; to distract myself, but it didn't help. "ZAYN, WHERE ARE YOU?" I yell at the top of my lungs. "I'm coming!" I yell but as soon as I opened the door. He was standing there, "No! Not Now, get in!" He ordered pushing me inside the room and closing the door. "I hate you." I say loud enough for him to hear.

"I love you too, babe." He said trying to annoy me. I rolled my eyes at his comment, even though he can't see me.

more couple minutes later

"Malik! If you don't open the fucking door, I'll jump out the window!" I scream. The door suddenly opened, "Don't!" He paused. "Do that!" He finished. "I need to get out of here!" I tell him. "Just give to more seconds." He pleaded with his puppy eyes, which I couldn't resist. "Okay, but hurry up!" I tell him, he nods and rushes out of the room again.

And before I could sit on the bed, Zayn called me, "Mariam! I'm done. Please come to the roof."

"Coming!" I say running.

I raced up the stairs, and what I saw mad me speechless. "Wow!" was all I could say.

"What do you think?" Zayn smiles swung his arm around my waist. "It's amazing!" I say admiring the view.

There was a picnic basket, under it was a sheet, where we could sit. On the other side of the roof, there was a small stereo and two sleeping bags. Other than that, the place was filled with red roses and white daises. I turned around to face Zayn. But before I could thank him, his lips caught mine. I kissed back. But he pulled away, and smirked. "Let's leave the best for the end." He whispers in my ear. "What a shame." I smirk. "I had a lot planned." I say and Zayn opens his mouth. "I just wish you could keep your pants on." Zayn stares at me, shocked. I smirk.

....

Please vote and comment

Thanks

Chapter 16

- -

I open my eyes slowly, as I try my best not to cry. I was hiding behind his bed, in his bedroom that he locked me in for who knows how long. He'll come for me, I'm sure he will. He will beat me up until I pass out again. My breathing was messed up. "Mariam." He calls. I'm going to faint, everything is spinning, my body is shaking badly and I'm sweating a lot. "Please don't hurt me." I beg him. "You did something wrong, and you must be punished." He told me, coldly. I tried to take breath, "I am never meant to burn your shirt, please." Tears spilled out of my eyes.

"You better come out before I find you, or trust me, I will beat you up like worthless dog." He spats harshly, making me tremble. Shakily, I get out of my hiding spot to see him there, standing in the middle of the room with a black leather belt in his left hand. "Come here." He demands angrily. I walk towards him, knowing that this pain will be unbearable. His fist made contact with my jaw, making me fall back wards.

"I'm so sorry. I'm very sorry. I'll buy you a new shirt. Just please, stop." I curl up into a ball.

"No! You did something wrong, and you deserve a fucking punishment!" He groaned.

He rained his black belt on my body so many times that I lost count. "You are stupid, worthless and carefree." He hit me after each word that he spat with venom.

"You ruin everything that makes me happy."

"I di-" A hand made contact with my cheek, making shut up.

"Shut up! You think you can ruin my favorite shirt, ruin my night with my friends and talk back at me?" He yells at me.

"P-please.." I stutter.

He grabbed a fistful of my hair and he banged my head against the wall a couple of times, until my head was bleeding. Then he let go, but grabbed my neck. "Pl-eas-e.." I was running out of breath as his grip tightened.

Everything was turning to a darker shade when he let go of my neck and my fragile body falls to the floor, motionless. He walked towards his beside table and opened the drawer, he gets out a gun!

"W-what a-re y-you goi-ng t-to do?" I try to make words.

"I'll do the thing I wanted to do for years, I'll end my source of misery. I'll kill you." He says emotionlessly. I was trembling with fear. He fixed the gun in my direction, my breathing was completely gone and my face was white! He placed his index finger on the tigger. "I beg you don't." I cry. I felt a major pain in my head.

Then 'BANG!' was all I heard. I gathered all the power left in me and let out a blood piercing scream.

*

*

"Mariam! Mariam! What's wrong?" I hear someone screaming. I opened my eyes and saw Zayn. I kept staring at him, trying to understand what happened.

"Why were you screaming?" He asked with worry lacing his broken voice.

"I-I had a nightmare." A tear spilled out of my eye.

Zayn just stared at me, then grabbed me and pressed me against his muscular chest. I couldn't move, I wasn't able to hug him back, this nightmare seemed so real and so true. "Mariam, you are very cold." Zayn states as he touches my hand. Soon Zayn also noticed I was shaking. "E-everything seemed s-so real." I cry into his chest.

"I'll go get you cup of water." Zayn gave me a warm smile. I was shaking terribly. "Zayn, please don't leave me." I sob into my knees since Zayn let go of me. He didn't hear me, Zayn walked away. "I will kill you." I heard someone whisper to me. I looked up, out of my knees and still the was nobody there. "Zayn!!" I shake even more.

"What? Is anything wrong-" Zayn suddenly stops talking as if he saw a ghost. "Z-zayn?" I question. "Mariam, you are white! You're face is fucking white! What happened?" Zayn says quickly. "I-I-" I run out of breath and everything turned all black.

*

*

Weakly, I flutter my eyes open. I saw five boys. "Mariam!" Zayn yells hugging me. "I was so fucking worried." He cried. Harry gave a weak smile. "What happened to you?" Niall asked me. "Yeah, you look like you have seen a ghost." Liam states shocked. "Zayn scared us; he told us that your face was very pale and your body was so cold." Louis said biting his lower lip.

"I just felt sick. I'm sorry that Zayn is overdramatic-" I wanted them to feel like it's not a big deal, but sadly I couldn't. "Overdramatic!" Zayn rephrases.

"You weren't breathing! I splashed water all over your face almost ten times, and you didn't even move. How could I be fucking 'overdramatic'?".

I felt a sharp pain in my head again. "Owe." I say placing a hand on my forehead. "Here! Take this." Niall gave me a small pink tablet and a cup of water. "Thank you." I thanked him as I took them from him and swallowed the tablet.

I did feel better, but that nightmare was killing me and I don't know weather should I tell anyone or not!

"Are you better now?" Harry shots at me. I gave him a quick nod in response. "I think you should rest now." Harry suggested. I shook my head at once. "Okay?" Harry hesitated. "Zayn!" Harry yelled. "Yes?" He answered. "I need to talk to you." He told him. I don't know why but I really don't have good feeling about whatever they are going to discuss. But anyways I have bigger problems right now, like this nightmare! What if I keep having more nightmares, I'll never be able to sleep again.

I think I should tell Zayn...

....

Please vote and comment

Thanks

Chapter 17

I haven't told Zayn about anything yet; I'm so scared. I don't know how will he react. What will happen if he told Harry??

'Oh god! No, I can't do that!'.

"Mariam? Are you sure you're okay?" Zayn asks looking at my pale, yellow face. "I-I am." I glup.

"Well, I better start getting dressed for school, ain't that right?" I pop my head up, looking at Niall, hoping he would help me. "Yeah, sure!!" He said awkwardly. 'Good acting Nialler!' Note the sarcasm.

After the boys got out of the room, 'Finally!' I sign, I throw on whatever in front of me. I walked down and started making some cheese sandwiches for me and the boys. I was finished with food. "Hey!! Guys breakfast is ready!" I shout. And they all rushed into the kitchen. "Have you ever eaten before?" I sassed and Liam just looked at me and gave me the 'What the hell I am hungry?' Look.

I'm almost finished my sandwish, but the boys were already done, 'Am I that slow?!'. "Mariam, are you going to finish tomorrow?" Louis said then laughed like crazy at his own joke. "All I could tell you Louis, is that you are pathetic." I tell him. "And you're mean!" He screams as he fake cries. I roll my eyes at his stupid act. "Guys, you could go to the school now. Mariam and I have late periods today, so we are gonna be late." Zayn announces. "Okay, mate. See you later." Liam says. "Bye!" Louis yells. "Bye." I answer. "I'm not talking to you." He sticks his tongue at me. I roll my eyes.

*

*

"Zayn! We are gonna be fucking late!" I yell. "I'm coming!" He yells back. I jumped in his black BMW. "Wow." I mumble. "Happy you like it. I guess we have the same taste in everything." Zayn smirked. "N-no!" I say as my cheeks turn into a deep shade of red. "I mean I like-" I couldn't from words. "Could you search for my sun sunglasses?" Zayn asks. "I don't really think you need it." I sass. "C'mon babe." I can't help but blush at his extremely sexy British accent.

I can see his hot smirk, spread across his face. "Fine." I roll my eyes. I looked for them in the car's drawer. And something else caught my eyes. It had a huge 'Mariam ♥' written on it. "Zayn, what is this?" I couldn't stop myself, but curiosity was killing me. "Why don't you open it and see?" Zayn suggested. "No need to tell me twice." I say opening the envelop. I opened the envelop and started reading it.

I knew you wouldn't be able to hold yourself. I knew you would be so curious about that letter, that had your name on it. But don't feel bad or anything. I mean who wouldn't wanna open a letter with his name on it. Well I would too . Anyways, I wanted to talk about something more important, it is my love to you ♥. And please try to help me cuz I suck at these kinda things . I have always felt a special connection between me and you, it felt like stars . I couldn't sleep , eat or think , without you. Mariam, you are my everything. You made me feel things I never felt before and I'm sure also things, that I'll never feel without you ♥. Please always stay by my side . Cause no matter what comes between us I will always love you . Will you be my girl?

Your's one and only love, Zayn .

I was speechless. "What do you say, babe?" He said in his husky voice. Zayn stopped the car in the school's parking lot. I nod, Zayn smiled as he turned to me. "Really?" He says, jumping up and down from excitement. "Yes. Yes. Yes!" I yell. But soon I was stopped by Zayn crashing his lips to mine. Our lips danced in sync as we made out. "I love you." I mumble through the making out session. "I love you, even more." He kissed me harder.

*

*

But still, I was sure 100% sure, that if Harry found out, he will kill both of us. So I was kind of a little bit-okay! a lot, 'concerned' about what will Harry think about this.

As we got to the school, I kept a little distance between me and Zayn so Harry won't notice. But Zayn, on the other hand, looked pretty annoyed by my actions; like when he tried to hold my hand, I moved away. Today I had all periods on my own, except for one which was with Zayn.

'Great!' You think, huh?

'Well if you thought that you're wrong! Cause Harry is with us.'

Skipping most of the lessons

It is now break time and I am sitting with boys. When out of the blue, I noticed that I forgot my mobile in my locker. "I am gonna go get my mobile from my locker, I'll be back in a second." I said, excusing myself. "Want me to come with you?" Zayn asked. "No, its fine. Thanks." I replied. As I walked to my locker, I met Payton and Trish with their minions. "Hey bitch." Payton screamed at me. I walked away and tried to ignore them as best as I can but I felt someone pull my hair and it brought me to the floor. "Oww, You bitch!" I scream as I turn back to face them.

Trish wad behind me, smirking. "What did you just say?" Payton yelled as she stepped on my hand. Tears started falling from my eyes, when someone appeared in front of me. "Leave her Payton!" A girl voice boomed, I looked at her I never saw her before I guess she is new here.

"Oh, hey loser! Wanna join your worthless friend?" Payton mocked and then Harry appeared which made me sigh in relief. "Payton! Stay away from her now!" Harry screamed and Payton looked really shocked.

"Harry, baby are you drunk?" She asked leaning her body on him. "Payton, stay away from me and my sister. I can't deal with this anymore." He yells at her. She looked scared and walked away while the girl who defended me, ran towards my aid and helped me up. "Are you alright?" she asked worriedly. "Yeah thanks." I thanked. "I am Nouran." She greeted, placing a hand in front of me to shake. "I am Mariam." I replied and shook her hand.

Then Harry rushed over to me "Hey, are you okay?" Niall asked looking worried. " Don't worry, I am fine." I said smiling then Harry was staring at Nouran. "Oh, Harry, this is Nouran," I introduced them to each other, and they both shook hands. "Well Nouran, this is my brother." I said pointing to Harry.

"It was really nice meeting you, but I must go; I have a lesson now." She said giving me a warm smile. "It's okay, bye. Hope to see you soon." I said to her as we walked away and waved goodbye.

And the bell rang, "Great!" I huffed. I walked to my locker and got my mobile and books, I had Math with Harry and Zayn. "I guess this will be fun." I mumbled, sarcastically to myself. I shut my locker and walk to Math class.

I was the only one there until Nouran showed up, and automatically, my face lit up. Hey, we have same class!" I said smiling like a child. "Yay!" she cheered. "Would you sit next to me?" She asked.

One thing popped in my mind, which was 'Zayn. Will. Kill. Me.'

"Yeah. Sure." I said, ignoring my thoughts. I sat there and we chatted for a bit, we told each other and I found out that she isn't a new student but she transferred here a year ago.

Then hell started, formally known as Math lessons.

Everyone was in the class, including Zayn and to make it better, Harry was sitting behind me. "Mariam, are you sure you're okay?" Harry whispered to me. But Mr Jack noticed. "Mariam and Harry, would you care to tell us what were you both talking about, that is so serious, that you both are talking about in my lesson?" Mr Jack screamed. I rolled my eye. I was like 'Chill dude.' that's what I really wanted to say. But I don't have the fucking guts to.

"Well since both don't have anything to say, I think the three of us could discuss, later in the detention." He smiles in victory. "Fuck you." I mumbled. "What was that, Miss Mariam?"

"Nothing, Mr Jack. May I have a seat?" I ask politely in a bitter sweet way.

"Nope." He says and turns back to teaching.

'Fine asshole, I'll play your fucking game as well.'

As soon as he turned around I pulled his chair away. He didn't fucking notice!

Oh my god, this guy needs new glasses. I was about to explode from laughter.

Then it's the time when was about to sit. He fell on his arse in front of the whole class. "Shit!" I breakdown laughing my ass off. "Mariam, out now!" He roared. I obeyed him and got out but still laughing so hard.

....

Please vote and comment

Thanks

Chapter 18

"Yes, dad. I swear it was nothing serious-I was just having a little fun at class. Okay-okay I'll take care next time. Okay dad. Fine. Bye. Love you too." I hung up.

'Yes, of course Mr Jack-ass called my father.'

*

*

"Hey! Zayn!!" I yelled like a four year old. "Yes babe?" He answers making me melt. "Can we do sleepover?" I say jumping up and down. "But we are already kinda living in them house? Hell, even the same room." Zayn says in the form of a question. "No, silly. I meant you could invite the boys over and I'll invite Nouran." I explain. "Okay, and maybe we could paint our nail and do makeovers." Zayn mocks. "Of course, Zayniee!"

"I hate you." He huffs. "I could tell the boys to bring their girlfriends too if you wan-" I interrupted Zayn. "Girlfriends? Since when does the boys have girlfriends?" I was surprised. "Since a lot." Zayn smirks. "Ha. Ha. Ha." I laugh. "Okay, tell them to bring them." I sass as I swing my hips walking away. "Where do you think you're going?" Zayn asks. "To my room." I say in a 'duh' tone. "Not so fast Miss," he says. "Before I call the guys I need something in return." He grins "What do yo-" I didn't get to finish my sentence cause Zayn's tongue was down my throat.

*

*

"Okay, I'll see you at 8." I say. "Bye." I say as I hang up with Nouran. I walked to the kitchen to see Zayn, making food as he was singing in a low voice. "Hey, what are you doing babe?" I asked "Just making us dinner." He replied. "Oh well, but I heard you singing as well." I said as his face turned tomato red. "You have a great voice, you should sing more; I love it and you sound so sexy." I bite my lower lip. "Thanks babe." He thanked as pushed his lips against mine.

*

*

The door bell rang, "They are here, yay." Zayn said sarcastically. "Please low down the enthusiasm." I roll my eyes as I get up and headed towards the door. "Hey!" I greet them all, even the faces I don't know. "Hello." Harry greets. "Hi," Louis says. "So let me introduce you to everyone, This is Eleanor, my girlfriend. This is Sophia, Liam's girlfriend and finally this is Perrie, she is Sophia's friend. We hope you don't mind she tagged along." Louis says to me. "No, not at all." I shot at her a welcoming smile and she smiled back.

We all decided to play truth or dare. So we sat on the ground and got a bottle, and spined it till it stopped at Louis and Zayn. "Well Zayn, truth or dare?" Louis asked smirking. "Dare!" Zayn said confidentially. "Okay, I dare you to go with anyone sitting next to you and make out for five minutes in the bathroom." Louis smiled evilly.

I was sitting next to him but on the other side there sat Perrie.

Zayn looked to me and we both had the same idea, but Harry was giving Zayn a death glare "Don't even think about it." Harry whispered to Zayn.

Zayn backed away and then looked at Perrie and she said "Okay." As she smirked at me. Both, Zayn and Perrie walked to the bathroom and they closed the door. In that moment I felt anger boil up inside me, I couldn't believe that Zayn is making out with another girl.

"Hey, you look pissed. Did something happen?" Nouran asked me noticing I was angry. It's just Za-" I was cut off when Zayn and Perrie came out both laughing I was about to explode. "Bitch." I mumbled as Perrie passed by me. Perrie gave me another stupid smirk and then she excused herself to go get water we spined the bottle again and it stopped at me and Sophia "What would you choose? "Dare." I smirk. "Well then I dare you to kiss Niall a long French kiss." She said as my heart stopped Harry and Zayn were both glaring at me.

I stood up and walked over to him slowly and then our lips kissed. I can't lie; Niall is a great kisser, but I don't feel that spark when I kiss him. After about kissing for a couple minutes I felt two hands grabbing my hips backwards. I turned around to see a really angry Zayn. I walked back to my place. I actually think Zayn deserves me kissing Niall. He needs to feel how I felt while he was making out with Perrie. "Don't you ever do that again." Zayn whispered angrily "Then you stop too." I whispered back.

Then the devil came back with the water and while she was walking I felt a cold liquid fell over my body, everyone gasped as turned and saw Perrie. "Oops, I didn't see you there." She mocked. "Fuck you." I screamed and ran to my room.

Exactly two seconds letter there was a soft knock on the door. "Who is it?" I screamed. "Mariam, please let us in. It's only me and Harry." Nouran said softly, I walked to the door slowly and opened it and then closed it right after they walked in. "Oh my god! Mariam, you didn't change yet! you're gonna catch a cold! Get in the shower right now." Nouran said in a caring tone.

I was in the hot shower and then I saw my shaver's razors. I wasn't suicidal or anything but I was in so much pain and anger so grabbed it. A loud knock hit my door, making my hand shake and cut my wrist. "Ahh!" I scream. It was bleeding so badly. It stings so much.

After I was done. I put wrap a towel around my wrist. 'Stop fucking bleeding!' I panic. After it stopped a little.

Then I grabbed my PJs and walked to my bathroom and took a really quick bath, and then I got out. "What is this? Do you cut?" Harry asked as griped on my wrist. "Why did you do this?" Harry said a little bit starting to yell. "I-I-" I stuttered. "You what?" Harry yelled and I started tearing up. I didn't get a chance to explain what happened.

"Harry, please calm down! Give her take a break please."Nouran said as she broke Harry's grip from my wrist. "Okay, first of all, we need to stop the bleeding." Nouran said as she brought the first aid kit from my bathroom she wiped all the blood and then sprayed on it some alcohol so it is cleaned but it hurt like hell "Ouch." I wince. "Hold still." She said and as she applied some bandages to it. "Thank you." I said, she hugged me then I saw the door being pushed and appeared a worried Zayn. "What happened?" he asks anxiously.

"It's nothing, I-I just got hurt and-" I said "What? Where?" He asked "On my wrist." I mumbled and then I was brought to Zayn's chest. "Zayn, break it up, will you? That's enough boys for one day." Harry pulled me away from Zayn.

"I think we all need to rest, right now." Nouran said and we all nodded. Nouran and I slept as fast as we can cause today was a lot worse than I thought it would be but I hope tomorrow won't.

....

Please vote and comment

Thanks

Chapter 19

I walked out of bed and shook Nouran till she woke up, "Morning." I said as she semi-smiled and then fell asleep again. "Nouran, move your ass out of bed now!!" I screamed and she jumped in shock. "What the fuck Mariam? This is not a way to wake up a human." She said as she rubbed her eyes.

I walked downstairs and saw that everyone was still sleeping except Perrie, which leaves me, Nouran and the bitch. I walked to the kitchen and saw her sitting there at the kitchen's island "Sup?" she said as she saw me walking in I could have sworn she said 'Whore' in a low voice "Good." I said with an attitude.

"Whatever." She mumbled, I rolled my eyes at her. I was walking to the fridge when "Yeah Mariam, I need to tell you something." She smirked as she stood from her place and walked towards me.

"By the way, Zayn is mine, so back up bitch." She whispered into my ear as she pushed me, but I was already gonna explode, so I pulled her hair. She turned to me and pushed me so hard that my back hit the floor, then she jumped on me and she started scratching my face, slapping my cheek, punching my jaw and also pulling my hair.

I tried to stop her but she was fast until she stopped for a moment, so I pushed her back and jumped on her I pulled her hair again but because the wound on my wrist, my arms were so weak.

When I felt someone lifting me from my back I turned around and saw Zayn, with a shocked look on his face. "Mariam, what do you think you are doing?" He yelled, I opened my mouth for words to come out but nothing did. I just couldn't help it, some tears ran down my face and I took this chance to run to my room. I can't stay here any longer.

I have had enough with this stupid drama. "Mariam, what are you doing?" Nouran asked. "I I-I am going for a walk." I said as I changed into my skinny jeans and threw on my red t-shirt and red vans I grabbed my bag and my mobile phone my earphones and ran out of the house I ran to the park which is near my house and sat there for a while, trying to relax or even breathe. I pushed my hands up to face and cried silently until I heard laughter, I looked slowly to see Payton and Trish and there is another figure behind them but I can't make out who is he?

"Why are you crying, slut?" Payton mocked me. "Non of your fucking business." I dry my tears as I was about to move up but then the figure from behind walked towards me and held me back to the bench I was sitting at. "What the fuck! let go of me!" I screamed, but he just smirked.

I felt him push my back harder, which was so painful just like what Louis did to me before, I winced in pain, when Payton started talking again. "As you can see Nathan, here. He is my new boyfriend and he is better than your dumbass brother, who fucking dumped me for you." she looked disgusted. "Shut the fu-" before I can even continue, I felt a strong punch in my stomach. I can do nothing but to sit there and feel a lot of pain in my sore stomach.

"And also Nathan here, he can teach you good lesson about how not to steal other's boyfriends, don't you think too Trish?" She said playing with her ugly curled hair and Trish just nodded "Don't you think too Trish?" I mimicked her. Payton rolled her eyes and then I felt being pulled Nathan kept pulling me but I tried to stop him with all my strength. "Let go of me right now or I will scream." I threatened Nathan which made things even worse he gave me a death glare and then moved closer to me.

"I would love to see you try." He whispered in my ear, sending chills down my spine. I just nodded. I couldn't believe that my old bullying life have ended just for a new one to start.

Does the universe hate me or what?

Nathan shoved me aside and kept dragging me to who knows where.

I kept squirming but that didn't help at all, actually all he did was tighten his grip even more. I guess we were at the back of some abandoned building he pined me to its wall. "Well I am not like the boys, I know they used to take it easy on you but I won't." He smirked. He punched my gut a couple of times until I stopped counting. As he threw one more punch and I totally couldn't bare it any more. "Of course, if you disobey me there will be consequences. And I bet you don't wanna know them. So lets play good." He whispered to my ear and then he let me go.

"Well, I guess that's enough for today." He smirked and I wanted to hit him or fight back but I couldn't; I knew he would beat the hell out of me. I tried to run but I couldn't, "Please Nathan, stop." I cry but it totally meant nothing cause all I got was a black eye and that was the last thing I remember berfor I blacked out.

I limped all my way home. "Owee." My gut hurts so bad, that I'm feeling so sick, like I'm gonna throw up or something.

'Why does my life has to be like this?'

I opened the door and got in just to be greeted by worried and angry faces of the boys and Nouran. Thank god, Perrie wasn't here but neither was Sophia.

Nouran ran to me and gave me a hug. "Thank goodness you're okay." She said as she hugged me tightly. "Where the hell were you? Mariam, we were all worried sick about you." Harry yelled at me. "I was at the par-" I mumbled slowly. "What happened to your eye?!" Niall yelled. "I just fell and hurt my eye." I lied and tried to make a run for it. when I was held back by Zayn. "Let go of me!" I said as tears appeared on my face when Zayn saw me crying, and he let go of my wrist at once and I continued heading to my room.

I threw my bag on the floor and looked to the mirror I saw a stupid, pathetic, useless girl, looking really ugly with huge black eye on her face.

"I hate myself, I hate my looks, I hate my life, I am worthless, I don't do anything in my life other than cry and cry." I lifted my T-shirt and saw my purple and blue stomach, "I guess Nathan is a lot tougher than I thought." I mumbled. My thoughts were interrupted when "Who's Nathan?" My heart stopped, I guess I said that out loud! I turned around and saw Nouran. "So who is he?" She repeats. "He's-nobody." I smile trying to cover up what I just said.

....

Please vote and comment

Thanks

Chapter 20

I turned around and saw Nouran "Who's Nathan?" She repeated. "He is......" I try to make proper words but fail.

"Hmm..." Nouran hummed signaling me to continue. "He is a guy." I said.

I am so stupid, Nouran looked at me with a 'Really?' look. "Oh god! He is a guy! Really? Cause I thought he was a dog." she mocks. "Look, I am sorry but I can't tell you, okay!" I said trying to avoid looking at her. "Why can't you tell me?" She asked getting angry. "I can't please Nour-" She cut me off "No, no, its okay to hide whatever you are hiding, from your best friend." She was totally pissed off.

She walked away really annoyed. My hands were glued to my face when I heard a knock on the door, I looked up I saw Zayn, standing there smiling over to me. I just I slammed my face in my hands again. He moved closer and I felt him sit beside me.

Zayn's POV:

I never saw Mariam this sad before, not even when I bullied her, I guess there is something really bad going on, and as a well a supportive boyfriend I need to be there for her. "Mariam!" She looked up to me again but this time with tears in her eyes and then hugged me. I held her to me, tightly. I felt her breaths on my neck. I slowly rubbed her back. "Mariam, stop crying. What happened? Why are you crying?" I asked.

Mariam's POV:

"Suddenly, everything, my whole life turned into hell. And it's hard to keep up with everything." I cried harder to his neck, as he rubbed my back. It made me feel better. I really wished, I could tell him the whole truth, tell him, why was I crying, but I will look like I am a spoiled brat and attention seeker. Also Nathan threatened me not to tell anyone.

"I am sure, everything will be alright soon." As he kisses my forehead. I look deeply into his hazel eyes. "Really? You think so?" I ask. "I know so."

I cracked a teary smile. "Finally! I needed to see you smile." He shouted as he peeked my cheeks. "Thank you for being always there for me." I thanked him as I wipped my tears away.

"It's nothing and I want you to know, that you can tell me anything, but I want you to promise me, you'll never cry again." I nodded. "Cause, you look so pretty when you smile." He whispered softly. I never knew Zayn had this side of him, the side where he could always shower you with compliments and kisses; the only side I used to know the one who rains punches and kicks to your stomach.

"Let's go down and see whatever happened between you and Nouran." He dragged me out of my room.

We walked down and I saw Nouran was a bit hurt but Harry was standing next to her and hugging her.

'Wow, I didn't see that coming.'

Zayn kept dragging me towards her until Harry and Nouran noticed they were hugging. "I guess Harry is flirting with your best friend." Zayn nudged my arm, I gave him a blank look to act stupid and we walked to them.

"Ehmm." I coughed and both Harry and Nouran looked at me widen eyes. "Em Nouran, look I am really sorry please forgive me." I said fast, jumping on her and pulling her to suffocating hug.

she gave me a side smile and pulled me hugged back. "I forgive you." she mumbled in my ear. "I love you." I said. "I hate you." she hugged me tighter. "Okay, stop you two lesbians now that's enough." Louis joked or kind of tried to, as he entered the kitchen. But Harry was dying with laughter. "Haha, so funny. I'm dying with laughter." I mocked, Zayn smirked and I rolled my eyes. "Hey guys, don't wanna break your drama, but when are we gonna eat? I'm dying?" Niall whine.

"Okay, we could all go out and eat in McDonald's, maybe?" I suggested. "I think it's a great idea." Niall hopped in our conversation. We all threw on shoes and walked down the street.

*

*

We had a great time there, we were all stuffed. I really enjoy hanging out with them.

I never thought my life would be happy someday, actually that day of me hanging out with my ex-bullies and my bff is just hard to imagine, but what is really even more hard to even think about that I am dating on them and one of them.

When we got home I walked up with Nouran to my room and I changed in the bathroom while she was changing in the closet I finished and I was a ready in my PJs so as Nouran and we headed down to eat a snack we sat at the kitchen's island. "So how was your day with Harry?" I smirked her cheeks turned rosie pink.

"My what?"

"It was too oblivious that both of you were sharing something; the way he kept looking at you and the way you looked at him back in the restaurant." My smirk even grew wider.

"I-it was nothing!" she exclaimed,

"You're blushing." I waved my eyebrows at her.

"Okay, fine. I do think he is- I mean he might be sexy." She admitted. And I smirked in victory.

"Happy now?" she pouted.

"Better than ev-" I was cut off when Harry entered the kitchen looking at us.

Nouran's POV:

I felt my heart stop!

'Did he hear me?'

I am gonna commit suicide right now. I need a knife! I feel it is harder to breathe, every second that he is here.

'Why isn't he talking?' I guess he heard us, I am totally gonna kill Mariam! She is the fucking reason, I am in this shit. I wanna scream, right now! God, please say he didn't hear us.

....

Please vote and comment

Thanks

Chapter 21

'Please say you didn't hear me, please I am gonna die! And Mariam is just standing there smirking like stupid!'

"So girls, may I ask you a question?" Harry asked. "Yeah, sure." I replied quietly. "Does any of you has a date for the Graduation party?" He asks. I totally forgot about it! "Shit!" I mumble. "I'll take that as a 'no'." Harry smirks. "I do have." Mariam announced and Harry looked at her confused. "Well, who is he?" He shots curiously.

"You will find out soon." she says as she clicks his nose. He look a little pissed. "Okay, bye. I am heading to bed." Mariam yawned and walked towards the door. she winked at me, secretly but thank god, Harry didn't notice.

"So why don't you have a date?" He asks me, and blush uncontrollably. "Me, well, maybe-erm." I reply quickly. He stops me as he speaks.

"How come a beautiful girl like you doesn't have a boyfriend?"

"Beautiful? You think I am beautiful?" I choke on my saliva.

"Wanna go with me? I am free." He smirks.

"I'll think about it." I sass.

"Okay kitten, I'll pick you up at nine." He whispered in my ears. My eyes widened open, "Goodnight." He says as he walks out of the kitchen. "Goodnight." I mumbled back in a low voice, and I am sure a %100 he didn't hear me.

I walk to Mariam's room, I opened the door and got in, when I turned around to close the door. "What did he say?" I hear a voice from behind me, I turn and see Mariam sitting on the bed. "Didn't you say you wanna sleep?" I ask. "I am a good actor, hold your applause." She says, proudly. I roll my eyes.

"Okay, he asked me to go with him." I say as a big smile appeared on my face. and I can't help but smile from happiness so this is what is love like, it is pure and beautiful.

I threw myself at Mariam's bed "Congrats!" Mariam whisper screamed. "Goodnight." I say "Goodnight." she replies.

*

The next day (the day before the GP)

*

Mariam's POV:

I woke up and saw Nouran next me asleep, I was so happy Harry asked her to be his date. Still one person I am waiting to ask me.

"Nouran, wake up! It's an emergency!" I scream. "What happened?" she asks, half asleep. "We didn't buy our dresses for the graduation party." I say sadly, in a playfully way, she picks up her pillow and throws it at me. "Hey!" I whine. "You deserve it." She sasses.

"Oh no, you are playing with wrong girl." I fight. "We will see about that." she picks up her pillow again and I pick up mine. "War starts in 3, 2," I say "1!" She screams. We both keep hitting each other till we are of breath and then we fall on the bed both of us giggling. "I won, bitch!" I squealed "No, hoe. I did." She argued. "Nope, me! You're just jealous." I say "Whatever, you say Miss sass."

"Thank you, that was a nice compliment." I say in a classic way and then we both end up laughing again.

I walked up to the bathroom but she raced me too it. "I got here first, so you can wait at the back of the line." she says and then closes the door. "Open the fucking door right now!" I boom, but she doesn't answer. "Okay, two can play this game." I say as walked to the kitchen.

I turned off the hot water and giggled, imaging she look like a piece of ice by then. "Mariam!!" Nouran screams. "Yes?" I answer politely as I walk to my room. "Y-you little bitch, you switched the hot water off-f." She stuttered, shivering and I nodded proudly.

She was only in a towel around her body and I was dying from laughter. "Hey, what's going on? What is so funn-" Harry was cut off when he saw Nouran in a towel and Nouran's cheeks turned tomato red.

And this made me laugh even more that fell on the floor. "That's it!" She says trying to hide her red cheeks. She rushes out of the room.

"Well, that was awkward.." Harry says out of no where. "I think it was kind of funny." I say still giggling, I was filled with laughter. "So what are you gonna do today?" I ask Harry after finally finishing laughter. "I am gonna pack my things and go home right now and then me and the boys will go buy our tuxedos and then I am gonna pick up Nouran." He smiles at the thought of her name. He definitely likes her.

"So is your mysterious date gonna pick you up?" He asks. "Yup." I nod. 'As soon as he asks me for prom first.' I say in my head.

"Good. He better take care of you, or I will beat the hell out of him." Harry says protectively, I smile in response. "I pull him into a huge hug, as he hugged me back. "But I am sure, you will be great friends." I say.

'Or you are actually friends.' I laugh internally. I didn't say that part out loud.

"Okay, bye now. I will miss you." I say. "Me too." He says as he peaks my cheek and walks down to the living room, to start packing.

Then the door is pushed open and I see Nouran's angry face. "Well, well, nice to see you." I say as I start giggling again. "Oh stop, and go get your fat ass ready; we have a long day ahead of us." She says as she pushes me around, playfully. I stick out my tongue at her, then go in my room and I get out black ripped jeans with white top and a black and white jacket and my maroon vans.

*

*

I saw all the boys are done packing and all of them are at the door. I run to Harry and hug him. "Bye." I say as I look in his green orbs and smile. "Bye." He kisses my forehead. "Bye, Zayn." I wave as he smile at me and I can't help but blush.

"C'mon!" I yell at Nouran as I pulled her to the car. "May I drive?" I beg with my puppy eyes. "No!" She says in a 'duhhh!' Tone. "pwease!" I say. "Okay.." she sighs. "Yay!" I yell and sit in the driver seat. The whole ride, Nouran and I were singing, not mention that we were about to die, twice!

*

*

We parked the car and got in the mall, and Nouran ran, dragging me behind her. She saw a beautiful long blue dress. I, myself, think it looked amazing and specially on her. I mean she had a great body and her skin color will totally match the dress. We walked in the shop and I was admiring the dresses when "Hey, Mariam! C'mon let's go get our hair done." She yelled dragging me.

"But what about my dress?" I say. "I bought you one but I want it to be a surprise." She says to me and I pout. I know it is really kind of her to do that. but I mean I need to see its color and try it on and what if it doesn't fit me? This will be embarrassing. Just the thought of this makes me flinch.

We walked in a huge salon and we sat waiting for our turns and after what seemed forever, it was our turn finally. We both sat there like statues. After we were finished we both looked so Amazing; Nouran straightened her hair while I dyed it blond and it was a bit wavey, I loved it so much. We bought new jewelry, shoes and make up, and a lot of other things, which after that I couldn't walk, but I still wanted to drive.

We both jumped back in car but I was still imaging how will my dress look like but then we were going to the car. "Can I drive?!" I scream "Not a chance." She says. "Pwea-" Before I can continue. "No, Mariam, I don't wanna die! This is not on my to-do list." She says, "You're a meanie!" I whine. "Oh, cut the crap; I am saving your ass and me from death." She says "Whatever." I roll my eyes.

The ride all was singing. And when we got home, we both didn't stop watching make up videos until I think now we can put make up with our eyes closed.

"I am tired." I yawn. "Me too." She says. "let's go to bed now." I suggested and she noded back. We walk to my room and we can barely walk after all this day. I throw my limp body on my bed so as Nouran and we both slept like babies.

The next day (GP DAY)

I jumped out of bed and I saw that Nouran wasn't there, already. I guess she woke up early today. I got to my bathroom and did my daily routine but finally for once my hair doesn't look so bad even after I slept with it. I will just redo some parts with my hair straightener. I did it up in a messy bun and walked down to eat my breakfast. "Good morning, sleepy head." Nouran says as she flips another pancake and places it on the my plate with the other one she already made, then she added some nutella chocolate to mine and two strawberries on the top as for her she added honey and some sugar on the top with some black berry and we both dug in.

"Wow! You are a great cook!" I say "Shanks." She smiles, with a mouth full of pancake. "Hey, may I now see my dress?" I ask "Nope! Wait, not now." She said sternly and I roll my eyes at her.

*

*

Before the GP with 3 hours

We were done with everything and then when we started to get ready. I finally got to see my dress and it was beautiful and after some time we were in our dresses and we were doing out make up and some other things like the jewelry, our hair etc......

Harry's POV:

I was in my tuxedo and I was done. I was going to pick up Nouran while Mariam's mysterious date will pick her up. I just hope today that nothing goes wrong. I drove off to my sister's house.

I got there, I walked out of my car and knocked on the door and it was Nouran who answered but she looked like a princess today, her make up and her dress suited her perfectly and her straight golden brown hair. I was speechless. I wanted to talk but nothing came out...

....

Please vote and comment. ❤

Thanks

Chapter 22

(This is how Nouran and Mariam looked like Nouran is the one on the left and Mariam is the one on the right)

I wanted to talk but nothing came out! "Eh..Hi." Which was all that I could squeak out. 'Stupid!' I yelled to myself, internally. "Hi Harry." She said

"Are you ready?" I ask. "Yeah, I am. Just gonna tell Mariam, I am going." she replied. "Hey Nouran, who's on the door?" Mariam asked and then she appeared, my mouth fell open "Wait is this is a joke?! There is no way you are Mariam, my sister!" I stated completely shocked.

Mariam raised her eyebrow "Gee thanks Harry." Mariam rolls her eyes. "Okay, when will your date pick you up?" I asked. "He texted and told me, he is on his way." She replied. "I really wanna know who is the lucky guy?" Nouran waves. "Wait! You don't know too!?" I was surprised. "No one knows but me and him." She tell us crossing my arms.

"Well have fun but don't do anything stupid." I say. "Okay, dad." She mocks. "Bye." Me and Nouran wave.

Mariam's POV:

And soon they disappered in the distance and then I felt I tap on my shoulder. "Missed me much?" Someone asked from behind I turned around and saw Zayn in a black tux and a rose tie. He looked so hot. "Of course." I say as I jumped on him "I am happy you did." He said, flawlessly.

(Zayn looked like he was in 'Night changes')

He looked at me while I did so too. Then in a moment our lips met and he kissed me. We kissed passionately and he held my body close to his but then we had to break up so we could breath. 'Fuck you air!'

"So let's go." He says "Sure." I nod I close my house's door which was open for what seemed forever and then I hoped in Zayn's car as he drove to our highschool and we soon got there. I got out of the car so did he and were holding hands.

The place was so crowded it was filled with people. Even more than the normal school days. I was scanning the people in the room then I noticed the boys, Liam Niall and Louis but Harry and Nouran aren't with them.

'Well I guess they are busy.' I smirk.

We both walk towards the boys and we greet them, "Hi." I wave. "Hey." They all chorused. Are you two togather?" Niall asked awkwardly. I just stayed quite while Zayn looked at me and smiled. His smile made me feel really comfortable and ehh-happy. "We are." I answered.

"If Harry found out, he is gonna be-" Louis says but I cut him off, "Amazed?" I say, more in the form of a question.

"Yes, amazed! I hope just not too amazed." Louis said the last part in a low voice but I still heard him well.

After exactly 2 minutes, we finally notice Nouran and Harry walking towards us. "Hi." Nouran waves to all of us and walked towards us.

"Wow, you look beautiful!" Niall says but then Harry glares at him and I laugh a little. "Thank you." Nouran thanks Niall. "Oh and Mariam where is your date?" Harry asked me. "He is right here." I say. "Where?" He asks again. "He is standing in front of you." I say and he his eyes head to Zayn. "What?!" Harry asked with a little bit of anger and surprise in his tone.

"We have been dating for some time." I say. Harry just breaths in and out and then,"Okay, fine! The most important thing is that you take care of her." Harry says pointing to Zayn, and Zayn nods, agreeing. Harry looks a little mad but then Nouran holds his hand and he smiles back at her.

A song boomed through the halls of the school and we all started dancing and having fun.

*

*

But after a lot time of dancing on pop music comes a slow song and then Zayn pulled my hand and I giggle.

I put both my hands on his shoulders while he holds my waist, and we both dance till the slow song is over. "Wanna get a drink?" Zayn winks and I nod. I know exactly what he's thinking.

"Zayn, we are in our graduation party. How the hell are you going to get alcohol?" I ask him as I lower my voice. "I have an idea." Zayn whispers in ear. He grabbed me and pulled me out of the highschool and were out in the parking lot. Zayn pulls a metal flask out of his suit's jacket. "Oh you look ready." I smirk. I take a sip of the flask and it tastes awful but then I get used to it. After maybe the third flask that Zayn gets from his car. I can barely see anymore. "Hey Zayn. I wanna go home; I am not feeling well." I say as he nods and helps me in the car.

He starts the car we drive home but I start to feel a little bit better, "Hey, are you sure you're okay on you your own?" Zayn asks me. "Yeah but if you wanna stay over it's okay nobody is coming here; Nouran took her things." I say to Zayn "Okay then." Zayn says and walks in we both totally were very drunk and we walked up to my room me and Zayn slid slowly under the covers.

The next day

I woke up I opened my eyes and saw Zayn sleeping next to me only one problem we both were naked my heart dropped.

'Did we just have-Oh no no no this can't happen at all! This wasn't what I wanted! I mean it is still early-oh please this can't be happening!'

I jump out of bed and have shower with all this thoughts still running in my head and then I put on my PJs but then suddenly my stomach hurts me. So much I ran to the bathroom and find myself throwing up. "God, please I can't be pregnant please this can't happen to me." I sob falling to the floor.

....

Hi guys what do you think of that?I hope you enjoyed this chapter.

Please vote and comment

Thanks

Chapter 23

I was still sobbing on the floor, when there was a knock on the bathroom door. "Mariam! Are you okay?" Zayn booms from behind the door. I wipe away my tears, I slowly stand up and walk over the door and unlock it Zayn is wearing only his boxer but I am thankful he is wearing them. "Are you okay?" He repeats, worriedly. "Yes, I am fine." I reply. "I-I just fell." I continue.

'*Cough* liar *cough*' I hear my conscious say at the back if my mind.

"Are you alright? Are you hurt?" He asks, worridly, analyzing my body. "No, no, I am fine. If you'll excuse me, I need to be somewhere." I say as I walk back to my room and I lock the door then I slide my back on the door slowly and then I fell to the ground. "What have I done?" I cry my stomach hurts me again.

Wait a second! This is maybe happening because I am a hungover! I stand up and throw on some jeans and a white t-shirt and I grab my phone as I am finished. I run out of the downstairs, hoping not to bump into Zayn, "Mariam, Wait!" Zayn yells from behind. "Yes, Zayn?" I answer him. "Do you need a ride; I can drive you if you want-" I cut him off, declining his offer. "No thanks; I'll walk." I rush out of the door.

I walk all the way to Nouran's house and Finally, I get there but my heart is beating so fast. I knocked on her door.

Nouran opened the door she look at me shocked. "What happened to you?" She asked. "Nouran, right now I will tell you something you must never ever tell anyone." I tell her.

"I promise you, I won't tell a soul." She promised. "Well yesterday after we got home from the graduation party, I-I offered Zayn to stay with me. And that was the last thing I remember." I start explaining.

"Today I wake up next to him and both of us were totally naked." I caught my breath because I was about to die and I was already crying and Nouran was trying to calm me a bit.

She seats me on her couch and sits next to me. "And today I wake up and my stomach hurts me so much and I guess." I was now fully sobbing and Nouran hugged me. "Calm down, calm down. I am going to buy you some pregnancy tests so we could put all of this non sense to bed." She says as she walks out of the door.

I am all alone and suddenly my mobile starts to ring. It's Zayn!

'What should I do??'

I won't pick up. A voice message starts to play after my phone started ringing. "Ehh-hello babe. Mariam, you were acting really weird-look I am so sorry-I don't remember anything from yesterday please-I swear. Please just answer my calls."

His voice seemed like it was about to break by the end of message and I was tearing up. "I am so sorry." I cry in low voice.

Then my mobile beeps.

Messages from Zaynie:

'Hello? Mariam?'

'Where are you? And why aren't you picking up?'

'You have been acting really strange all morning did something happen?'

'Mariam please pick up I am getting really worried'

I turn off my phone because the messages went on and on.

And then the door knob twisted and then Nouran enters. "Here." She says as she hands me the tests. I head towards the bathroom and after I am done and the answer is

Postive..I think

There was a fading second line.

"I am pregnant!" I cry.

"Don't worry, Mariam we will take care of the baby. I will always be there for you and I will help you no matter what but one question, are you planing to-you know tell Zayn?" Nouran asks.

"What?!" I practically scream.

"Well Mariam, after all he is the father of the baby." She points out, and she is 100% right.

"I know, I know but right now; it is so hard and I want it to stay like this for a while, please you promised." I sob.

"What about your family? Won't you tell them?" She asks again.

Then it struck me like lightning,"What will dad say about this?" I felt like my heart skipped a beat.

"Oh no, I feel sick again." I say placing a hand on my stomach.

"I am gonna call him." Cause this is probably guilt trying to kill me.

"Wait, what?" Nouran screams.

"I will." I can't keep secrets from him.

"Mariam, this is definitely a bad idea. And to be honest with you, you can't just spray this on him on the phone."

"You're right, I will tell him face to face, when I meet him. Cause telling him on the phone is the worst thing to ever do." I said to Nouran.

"Even worse than getting pregnant?" I sob to the floor.

"Okay, we will figure this out tomorrow, now go up to my room and rest; I will get you some food." She says and helps me up.

After I ate some sandwiches Nouran made me and then slept.

The next day

I heard a buzzing sound beside me I got up from my bed and and looked at the source from where the buzzing sound came and saw my mobile it was another message from Zayn.

'I missed you so much. Can we meet in the park next to your house? btw I moved back to my house but I really need to see you.'

'Ok' I text back.

I walk out of bed and walk down to see Nouran fell asleep on the couch I smile at how cute she looks when sleeping I take a blanket and cover her. I put on my shoe since I slept with my closthes yesterday and I get out and close the door behind me I take a cab to the park.

After I get there I see Zayn sitting alone, on a park bench. I walk towards him. "Hey." He waves I smile back at him. "So why did you leave in a sudden yesterday?" He asks. "Ehh...I had some errands to run." I lie "But you could have told me." Zayn argues. "I am sorry." I say "No, don't apologize. I am the one who is sorry, it is not even my place. " He frowns a little bit.

"Look Zayn, I am so sorry but right now there is alot running with my life and I need a little space if you wouldn't mind." I say hesitantly. "What!? Why is it something I did?" He asks with a broken tone. "Mariam, if it is because we had sex-I swear I was just as drunk as you were. I would never force you to do something you're uncomfortable wi-"

"No, Zayn- It's not tha-" He cuts me off. "Mariam, please don't go! I beg you. I can't afford to have you away from me please." Zayn was crying like actual tears.

My ex-Bully, Most popular guy in highschool, Zayn Javadd Malik was crying over of me. I couldn't take it anymore, I break down. "I am so sorry, Zayn but I need space." I cry. "Please!" He begs falling to his knees. "Zayn, please stand up. You're making a scene." I plead him. "Mariam, don't leave me." He cries louder. "I'm so sorry." I apologize as I walk away, terribly heart broken.

*

*

"Hey! Where were you?" Nouran asks "I was at the park with Zayn." I say "And did you tell him?" She asks.

" I told him that I needed space." I shake my head. "But right now, I am really scared; how am I gonna tell dad tomorrow, when he comes back?" I say as I almost cry.

"Don't worry, just calm down I am sure your father will be understanding." Nouran gives me a reassuring smile.

....

Please vote and comment

Thanks

HAPPY VALENTINES DAY

Btw Mine totally sucked; I broke up with my boyfriend today but actually I feel better now :) well I hope u had a good one.

Chapter 24

Just another day passed by which was hard for me, but well I actually a little part of me might be excited for the new baby; it is like mini me. I just hope he or she doesn't look like Zayn cause that will make it a lot harder to move on.

"Good morning." Nouran waves, waking me up from my thoughts.

"Morning." I say.

"Today is the big day; you're gonna tell your father." She announces.

"Yeah, you know what, I might be excited to have a baby of my own. I guess, he will approve, also don't you think?" I squeak.

"Yes! I actually thing he will. So hey, wanna a ride there?" Nouran asks.

"Yeah, thanks that would be great." I reply.

I stand up and walk towards the couch to collect my things. After I was done, we walk to the car, I sit in the passenger seat, next to Nouran, as we drive all the way to my house. After we got there, "Do you want me to go in there with you?" She offers. "Erm...No thank you, I guess I'll be fine. Just wish me luck." I say as I walk out of the car.

I look if there is there is any cars and then cross the road and open the door "Dad! Hello." I yell then a figure appears from the dark. "Princess." He yells as he hugs me and spins me around. "I missed you so much!" He stated as he puts me down. "Me too, daddy." I say.

"Daddy, I need to tell you something and it's really important." I say to him. "What is it?" He asks, calmly and completely not aware of what is going to hit him.

"Well," I take a deep breath and then let it out, "Dad, I am pregnant." I say as his smile turns into a frown.

"You're what?!" He yell as I back away "Da-d-dad." I stutter, shaking. "How could you?!" He screams at me with anger as I back away even more until my back hits the wall and he is walking even closer.

'What is he going to do? Is he gonna beat me again, like before? But wait if he does, he may hurt the baby!' A lot of crazy thoughts run through my mind.

"Dad! Wait, look if you want to beat me, please don't only this time because I am carring your grandchild and my baby so if anything happens to it, I will kill myself and even if you don't want to be part of it's life, it's fine. If you don't want to see me again, it's also fine!" I sob as my back slid down the cold wall.

Dad lifted his hand in the air, and I curled up in a ball and closed my eyes shut, I waited and waited but nothing happened. I opened my eyes and saw dad looking at me with so much anger and hatred.

"Dad, I am-" I was cut off by Dad. "Get out!" He roared, not even looking at me.

I felt my heart shatter. "NOW!" He yells louder, punching the wall beside me. I stepped back and walk towards the door. Everything was so blur. I cross, not looking at the road but then I heard a beeping coming from a near place but I continued to walk but then I was pushed to the ground and there was crash sound. Everything happened so fast, and I took a couple of seconds to connect the dots.

I turned around to see, Dad hit by a car. He pushed me so I wouldn't get hit by the car."D-Dad!" I say breathing heavely, Nouran runs out of the car and rushs towards us. "Daddy, please answer me!" I cry. "P-princess-ss, all I want you t-to d-do i-is take care of yourself and the baby please. Look I know, I haven't been the prefect father, but I love you, I swear I do." He says as he closes his eyes.

"No! No! No, dad please, don't leave me please!" I cry to his chest. "Daddy, I am so stupid, I wish I would go back and turn time only to stop this." I cry. Nouran called the ambulance and soon enough they were here.

Nouran and I were in the ambulance with dad while Nouran was calling Harry. After we arrived Dad was taken to the emergency room and I was crying my heart out and then suddenly, all five boys were here I run to Harry and hug him. "Harry, he-he is dying b-because of m-me." I cry to his chest and he holds me. "Mariam calm down. Breathe. Breathe." Harry says slowly. I held on to him like my life depended on it. He kissed my forehead.

"Harry, he is dying because of me, I am the reason he is here! If-if-f only I-" I was cut off by Harry. "Look Mariam, this isn't your fault, okay? Stop saying this." He hugs me, again.

Soon, Harry let's go of me and he sits next to me. "Mariam don't worry; we are all in this with you." Zayn smiles at me. "Thank you." I thank him and he hugs me immediately and then suddenly the nurse enters. "I have some news for you." She says, checking her clipboard.

....

Please vote and comment

Thanks ♥

Chapter 25

"I am sorry but he didn't make it." The nurse says sadly. I can't believe that my own father is dead because of me! "Wait, can we see him please?" Nouran asked her and she nodded. I walked and in and Nouran and the boys following us "Daddy! would-d you please wake up for me-e? I beg you!" I cry into his lifeless body. "Dad, please hold me; I need you." I sob as I slowly fall into the ground. "Mariam, I am sure if he was here, he would have held you in his arms and never let go of you." Nouran said as she hugged me.

Harry's POV:

I know I was the worst brother in the world even though I changed. And for the first time it breaking my heart to see her crying like that; she can't stop. I mean even when we used to beat her up, she never cried like this, in fact she always tried not to cry in front of us and at least in the past she was crying because of me. I mean I could have done something to stop it but this time I can do nothing about it but stand and watch my little sister suffer and I already know how hard it is to lose a parent imagine losing both I couldn't stand watching her like this.

"Mariam, please stop, crying isn't going to help." I said as I placed my hand on her shoulder. She turned around looked at me with eyes red from crying and they looked so pale and broken. I hugged her so tightly and she sobbed in my chest. Her cries are now more muffled and quiet. I rest my chin on her head.

Mariam's POV:

I sobbed into Harry's chest for what seemed for ever.

*

A few weeks later (after the funeral)

*

I was collecting my things from home, I need help taking care of the baby and I know who could help me. I am going to travel to New York City to my aunt Rachel. She is my father's cousin and she'll understand what I am going through. She'll take care of me and the baby. I mean hope so.

I continue collecting my things until I find a picture there was mom, dad and I, when I was 5. I felt tears coming to my eyes and they fell down my cheeks and I found a lot of memories that I missed. "At least you're both finally together, just like you always wanted." I cracked a weak smile.

After I was done, I took my bags and threw them in the corner invited the guys and Nouran here. They were gonna come in any minute now.

After 15 minutes exactly, they all were. I stood up and went to get door. The boys were all here so as Nouran. I let them in, "Hey.." I say trying to break the ice. "Hi." Louis and Zayn chorused in one tone. "Erm...I have some news." I say out of the blue. They all stared at me with their eyes wide open.

"Are they good or bad ones?" Liam asked worriedly. I didn't even tell Nouran "I-I don't know.." I stutter. "How don't you know?! It's either good or bad!" Harry shouted a bit."I'm going to go live with my aunt Rachel I am traveling to the U.S.A and I will live with her for a while." I say stuttering the last part.

They all looked at me shocked. "But why? You know we will always be by your side! Why do you need to go?!" Nouran said almost crying "I-I need to." I say as I look away. "Mariam, please don't go." I find Harry hugging me. "Harry, I can't, really. I need to I am so sorry." I apologize as I say good bye every and each one of them.

Then comes the hardest, Zayn one of all. We both were alone in the living room while the others were outside waiting for Zayn.

"Z-Zayn, I don't know how to say this but I need a little space, look I am so sorry but-" Zayn cut me off. "Wait wait! What? You are breaking up with me?!" He screamed.

"I am so sorry, Zayn." I say as I walk near him to hug him goodbye but he pushes me away. "Oww.." I whine. "I thought you need me too! I thought your feeling were true! But now you have proven me wrong. Goodbye Mariam." He spats with venom as he runs out of the house and by that today ended and today was the worst day of my life but at least tomorrow I am traveling I say to myself; hoping tomorrow will be better.

....

Please vote and comment

Thank you

Chapter 26

Mariam's POV:

"Mummy, Mummy, wake up now!" Maya said with her sweet voice. I open my eyes and find her staring at me with beautiful wide eyes. "You said you'll take me to the toy's store today." She said again and I laughed all at her little sweet voice.

Now, I am 23 and my little Maya is only 4. She has Zayn's brown eyes and my long bright brown hair she looks like a princess and she always reminds me of Zayn, which sometimes made me feel sad that she has to grow up away from her father.

"Okay just a second." I whine and close my eyes. "Mummyyy!!" She pouts.

I stand up and spin her around and she giggles with her cute laugh. I put her down and walk over to my closet and pick a maroon T-shirt and black ripped jeans with black vans and choose for Maya exactly the same I put my hair into a bun and so I did to hers. I kissed her baby pink cheek and she smiled at me. "Mummy, can you please wp?" She says and smile and lift her up and put her on my hip.

I grab my mobile and my wallet "Hey, Auntie Rachel. I'm going to buy a toy for Maya and coming home again." I yell. "Okay, dear." She answers back and I walk out with Maya on my hip. I put Maya in her seat next to me. She looked so excited. I sat in the driver seat and start driving.

Well as you can see after dad died, I moved to New York, with my aunt Rachel and I told her the truth, I told her everything from the every begging to the every end. My aunt knows every single detail about me. I work as stylist and I am trying to break into fashion industry.

But still at work I made a new friend called Fatima, and we greet each other and talk from time to time. She is amazing and I'm sure you're asking what about Nouran, well we fell out of touch, she become very busy with her job and she and Harry broke up, she told me it was for the best.

But I can't deny that I really miss her. I miss the old days, when I used to hang out with her and Harry, Niall, Liam ,Louis and even Zayn; I just sometimes miss my old life. I mean what if all of this never happened, what if I never got Maya? Would Dad would have still been alive and I would be still living with Dad, but I would have never known Fatima. I wish I could go to my old life, just for one second and say goodbye to everyone properly.

We arrived at the toy shop, I parked the car and got Maya out of her seat. and she jumped out of the car. "Yayyy!!" She screamed with excitement. I held her hand and walked in the store.

After 30 minutes of looking the perfect toy, that Maya thinks exists. "Maya, just choose one." I say, not feeling my legs anymore. "I don't know, they both look cute! Can I get them both?" She begs holding a Barbie and a Ken doll. "You know barbie is a princess so she probably needs a prince." She says, looking serious. I was dying from laughter from inside. "Fine." I huff as I roll my eyes. "Thank you, thank you, Mummy." She says as she hugs my legs.

We both walk out after we bought the barbie and Ken doll. "I'm gonna take care of you and Ken too!" she says talking to the dolls but then she starts running. "Wow, cute kittie!" She yelled running. "Maya, no wait!" I yell as I run after her but then she ran into and a stranger and fell on her bum. I run over there, "Hey, are you lost?" The tall man asks Maya. "No, I am her mother." I say. He looks at me and smiles, "Hello, sorry. I thought she was lost." He explains.

"No, it's okay." I smile back. "Oh, I am Ben. I work in magazines and modeling agencies." He introduces himself. "I am Mariam, it was nice meeting you, Ben. Hey, erm do you by any chance need a stylist?" I ask.

"Well, yes, I need some new stylists actually. If you would like to work for me that would be great." He says.

"Really?" I ask "Yes, here is my business card, if you need anything." He says handing me a small rectangular paper. "May I have your number?" He asks. "Oh, yeah sure" I say as I write it to him on a small paper. "Thank you, it was great to meet you." He says to me. "The pleasure is all mine." I say he walks off so as me and Maya. "You hear that baby, your mum is going to be a stylist! "I say spinning her around. "Yay, mummy sywist!." She cheers and I laugh.

*

*

I was sitting at home, not doing anything. Maya was sleeping and my aunt was going out with her friends. The my phone rang, breaking the cool air of quietness. I picked it up.

"Hello?" I answer. "Hey, Mariam, right?" He checks. "Well, I'm Ben, we met a couple of minutes ago." He announces. "Oh. Hey Ben-" He cuts me off before I could finish. "I landed you a job." He yells. "Oh my, really?" I ask excited. "Yup, you're going to be a make up artist for a preforming band, on tour." He states. "Thanks a lot, Ben." I thank him. "So I'll see you tomorrow in my office?" He asks. "Sure, but I don't have the addres-"

"It's written on my card."

"Okay, thanks, bye."

"Bye."

I hung up, jumping up and down. "I got a job!" I yell. But that means I'll have to leave my aunt and Maya. 'Oh, no way this will happen. I guess I have to just decline this perfect opportunity.

* Next day *

I was in the building, that his card lead me to, looking for Ben's office with Maya with me but she was in a bad mood because I woke her up from her beauty sleep. She is just so like a mini me.

I finally find office, written on it Ben White, so as written on the business card. I knock on the door. "Come in." Ben yells. I walk in with Maya. "Hey, I'm so delighted you could make it." He said "Well emm.. Ben look there is something I need to tell you, at least can I bring Maya with me on Tour?" I ask. "Sure can do!" He says "Well, now it time to meet the band, of course. You know the new boyband called one direction?" He asks.

"I might have heard their name before." I try to remember this familiar name.

Ben opens the door and reveals them and they stare at all me so as I analyze them as well but then I meet Zayn's eyes.

....

Please vote and comment

Thanks.

Chapter 27

Our eyes just met and I looked away as soon as they did. "Well Mariam, this is Harry, Liam, Niall, Louis and Zayn. They are also known as One Direction." Ben introduces then. "Yeah, we kn-know each other from before." I stutter as I look at the ground. "Really?" Ben says excited. "Yeah, we used to be friends in high school." Zayn says not even trying to look at me. "That's even better! More hot steamy drama!" Ben screams. "So boys sit down." He says as the boys sat next to each other on a couch.

"Mariam, the boys agreed you could bring another person with you but you need to travel in two days." Ben says.

"I agree." I say; I thought about it. My aunt doesn't work and lately, I couldn't find any jobs so we really need the money and I'll take Maya with me, so it's a great offer, which I couldn't refuse. I guess only it is gonna be deadly awkward and will bring up sad and hurting memories.

"Okay, then I'll leave you together so you could bring up memories." Ben says as he walks out of the office.

"Mummy, when will we go home?" Maya whines as they all stared at me eye widened. "M-Mummy?" Harry repeated shocked. "Erm.." I struggled to make proper words. "You adopted her, right?" Zayn asks. "Actually," I say as I look away quickly.

'Oh god, please don't make this awkward.' I pray inside my head.

*

Two days later

*I told my aunt everything, and she is happy for me but a little bit sad that she gets to stay all alone. I packed all my bags so as Maya's and now I am waiting for the van.

Zayn, Maya and I are the only ones there cause all of them are late, "Hi." Zayn said awkwardly, "Hello." I replied.

"Look, Mariam I don't want this to be awkward, so I am really sorry about what happened before but can we just open a fresh new start? Please?" He says. "Okay." I say. "I am sorry for breaking up with you too but suddenly all my life turned on me and everything was ha-" I was cut off.

"I don't want to talk about that, please." He says. "Okay, my bad." I say.

*

1 hour of awkwardness passed

*

Finally, everyone were there and the van came. I sat at the very back next to the window with Maya on my lap. Niall, Liam, Louis were in front of us while Harry sat next to the driver so I got stuck with Zayn sitting next to me but thank god the ride was quite and quick.

We got there and the house looked like a castle, it was so pretty and it had huge pool with garden that was full of flowers which Maya will love. I walked in and looked for my room.

"Okay guys, I am going to take the big room on the left on the second floor." I screamed walking to the room. "Okay." Louis yelled. I unpacked my things and Maya's and we're done. I walked down to the kitchen to eat something cause I was really hungry and Zayn was there.

'Lucky me!' I roll my eyes, mentally.

"Hey, Maya come with mummy to the kitchen?" I say to her. "Owky!" She says as she walks over to hold my finger with her tiny hand.

"Mommy, I want a sandwith (sandwich)!" She says cutely. "Okay princess." I say.

"Yeah, is it too late now to say sorry? Cause I'm missin more than just your body!" Zayn sang "You like Justin bieber?" I ask "Yeah! Very much actually." He says. "I hate hwm (him)." Maya comments out of no where. "He hit me and mummy!" Maya said which made me freak out.

Well cause I haven't told you about that part when I couldn't find a job so I dated a guy called Justin too, that's why Maya thinks he is the same guy.

'Me dating THE Justin Bieber, Lol.'

Anyway, My Justin-well actually my ex-Justin took care of me and Maya really well and he treated her like his own daughter but this is only because he treated me like his slave but that one day I wasn't in the mood for kissing that's when all the beating begun. He would beat me everyday but then he one day something happened, which made me couldn't stay with him anymore!

"Hit you and mummy!?!" Zayn repeated asking "Erm..I need to go!" I say as I walk away but Zayn grabs my wrist. "Mariam? Did someone hurt you?" Zayn asks worridly. "N-no!" I lie "Mariam, I know you're lying!" Zayn says. "No Zayn, I need to go." I say as tears run down my cheeks and he let's go of me immediately.

*

*

After some time all the boys decided to watch a movie and Liam was the one choosing and he chose Toy story 2 "Liam, remind me again how old are you?" I ask mockingly "Oh stop it and I actually chose it for Maya, you know!" He said totally lying. "Yeah right!" I said as I laughed. "I'll make us popcorn!" I announced and all the boys cheered. "I'll help you." Zayn said walking over to me. "Okay." I say, not even trying to stop him or complain.

"Me too, mummy!" Maya yells as she ran with her tiny feet.

We all walked over to the kitchen. I went over to and got the popcorn and placed it in the microwave. "So, Mariam" Zayn called. "Yes?" I answered. He sighed softly then spoke, "Look, I know that you don't want to talk about it and it's okay; this is your right. But all I just want to say is that you should talk to someone about this. This is something serious, Mariam." Zayn looked directly into my eyes.

"No I am fine-really-I-nothing happened!" I said trying to form proper words. "No, mummy remember when he hit you and you cry." Maya said which made my face turn red. "Yes, Maya. I totally forgot that! Thank you. Now, why don't you go and play princess?" I suggested. "Okay." she sang as she walked away "Nothing huh?" Zayn rolled his eyes. "Okay, okay. I'll tell you but promise never to tell anyone and specially Harry." I warn him. "I promise."

I sigh and start to explain, "It all started when I came here, I lived with my aunt. Everything was perfect until that one day, my aunt's lawyer died. She had a lot of debts and my poor aunt couldn't afford to pay them, so I started designing clothes, they got us money but not quite enough.

Then one night, I was at bar one day and met him Justin, he looked like a greek god, he had brownish-black eyes and wavy light brown hair. He was dancing when I bumped into him and kind of fell on him; I was deeply embarrassed. He was so perfect; I was speechless. It's like he casted a spell on me. I fell for him, I fell so hard that I didn't even realize it." I kind of felt sad for bringing back there old memories.

"The worst thing is I thought he loved me too. He was hot as hell, rich, and loved Maya; what could I probably want more."

"He promised to look after me and Maya which he actually did, but then he got betrayed by his best friend in their company and he became very aggressive. He would shout at me for completely no reason. Then one day he came so drunk and he wanted to have sex but I wasn't up for it. His face turned so red that I thought smoke might come out of his ears. He slapped me and this was when it all started happening, then second day he apologized then the next time I got pushed down the stairs then gotten apologized to again and the third time I got a whole beating-".

"Why did you stay?" Zayn asked placing his hand on my mine.

"I thought this was the best for Maya, she didn't know what was happening. He got her toys, candy and everything she wanted."

"I know that you love Maya but that is so wrong! And I'm sure if she knew what he did she have thrown all this away for you to be okay." Zayn words were the only thing I needed right now. I wanted someone to tell me that I did one right thing.

"Still you didn't say what made you leave him?"

"We got into a fight about but this time it ended up much worse, he beat me up until I wasn't even able to stand and I screamed by mistake from the pain, Maya rushed over to me and I wish I didn't." Tears started to form in my eyes because of this awful memory.

"He grabbed Maya and punched her in her stomach, and that was the last straw. I regained some power and pushed him and grabbed Maya ran out of there and I never retured back to him. I headed to the only place where I can go to, my aunt's. I told her everything and I had to stay in the hospital for some of time and that's pretty much all."

"Wow!" Zayn said his face expression shocked. "I can't believe you had to go through all of this on your own." Zayn pulled me in a huge bear hug.

"I wasn't on my own, I had my aunt and Maya." I whispered in his ear.

That's when BOOM!

Chapter 28

BOOM! I looked over to the microwave and opened it quickly."Oh god!" I said disgusted from the smell. "It got burned!" I say to Zayn. "Okay then throw it away and we will make another one." He smiled.

'God! How can he be so perfect?!' I thought to myself then snapped back to reality as I nodded quickly in response to Zayn.

"Zayn?" I called "Yes?" He replied so smoothly. "I don't think we have-" I was cutt off by Zayn smashing his lips into mine. The kiss was so passionate and I actually kissed back. I couldn't stop myself.

He held my waist and I held his neck, pulling me into him. Sadly, we broke up and Zayn half smiled, "Look in the upper cupboard." Zayn smirked. "Here!" He threw me a new pack and I placed it in the microwave and I was half sitting on the counter when Zayn came close, again. My mind was like HDIWKSJSLAKS!

"What was that?" I whisper/shout. "That's what you get for saying another guy if 'perfect' in front of me." He said in a challenging tone, he grinned. "Maybe it was a mistake." I said. "Whatever." He rolled his eyes and got out the popcorn. 'Thank god, it didn't burn again and then we returned to the living room.

"What took you so long?" Louis asked in a sheepish way and I gave him a blank look. "Yeah?" Niall asked with a mouth full of popcorn. "Well, the first got burned." I said. "Ah-ha!" Liam screamed! "What?" I asked, not understand his sudden outburst. "I knew you sucked at cooking! Harry, you owe me 20 bucks!" Liam laughed. "Harry, you bet on me?" I asked and they all laughed.

"Look who is taking? The geek." He mumbled but I heard him, "EX-CUSE ME!?" I sassed, "Nothing-ermm-i'm coming Harry!" Louis faked and walked out of the kitchen.

A few moments later and then I heard a noise behind me, "Louis, didn't you go already? Why are you back?" I sighed. "It's not Louis," someone said in an annoyed voice "It's Zayn." Zayn whined. "Yeah, whatever." I said, but then I felt Zayn place his arms around my waist, "Hey don't you think this is a little too close?" I raised my eyebrow at him, "No?" He said more in a question form. "No, Zayn get off me! Seriously, what if Harry saw you?" I lecture him.

"See what?" Harry asked entering the kitchen. "See that Zayn is preparing you a surprise!" I lied through my teeth, "Mariam please stop lying." He said annoyed. "Okay, fine." I signed.

"The truth is me and Zayn were preparing for you a cheese cake and I knew you loved them so I wanted to surprise you but now it's ruined." I huffed. "Aww," He awed at me "Thank you, sissy." Harry gives me a side hug. "I'll still act surprised though!" He squeaked as he walked away.

"Happy now you got me stuck making a cheese cake for Harry!" I crossed my arms playfully. "C'mon, I'll help you." He offered. "Okay." I huffed.

* Later that day *

"Why were you flirting with Nick?" Justin screamed at me as he threw an uncountable number of punches to me, but I was only crying, "I-I wasn't flirting with h-him, I s-swear." Tears run down my cheeks. "Oh! Do I look blind to you?" He screams and walked out of the kitchen and when I thought the torture was over.

I was wrong.

He came back, dragging Maya from her hair. "No-no please, leave Maya." I cry as she was screaming her little heart out. "Too late, should have thought of that earlier." He says as he simply smiled and kicked her head! He killed her! She completely stopped moving!

I couldn't hold back the pain I screamed my heart out.

*

*

"Ahh!" I screamed with all my power just to see that I'm in my bed. "It was a nightmare!" I mumbled in relief, placing a hand on my racing heart but when I looked next to me, Maya wasn't there! "Maya!" I called I was about to have a heart attack and then I got out of bed I walked around the house looking for balcony 'No' kitchen 'No' Living room 'No' Garden 'No' Pool 'No' Bathrooms 'No' "Maya!" I screamed and then, "Yes, Mummy!" She answered running towards me and I hugged her. "Where were you?" I asked as some tears fall down my face. "I was with Zi, I am sowwy, Mummy. I could not sweep, so I went to play with Zii!" She said happily. I was so relieved. "Mariam?" Zayn asked. I looked at him, "A-are you crying?" He asked I nodded. "Zayn, I had a nightmare about-" I cry and he hugged me and I felt secure for once.

"Zayn, it was horrible." I cried in his chest. "Not in front of Maya." He whispered in my ear and I nodded "Mummy, why are you crying?" She asked like she is about to cry.

"I just had a bad dream, baby." I said picking her up and she hugged me I started to rock her until she was sound asleep.

Zayn and I walked into my room with Maya in my arms but she is almost asleep. "So what was your nightmare about?" Zayn asked me. "It was about-t Justin, h-he started beating me until I was almost dead." I explain.

"He suddenly disappeared out of the room and then came back dragging Maya and kicked her until she bled to death, in front of my eyes and I couldn't do anything but watch her suffer." I cry and then Zayn jumped to hug me.

"Look as long as we all are alive, nobody could even think about touching you or Maya." Zayn assured me. "Thank you." I mumbled and He kissed my forehead. "Okay its getting late now, I guess I should go." Zayn said unhugging me.

"Wait, Zayn could you please stay with me," I asked in a low voice. "Only for the night?"

"Sure." He smiled.

....

Please vote and comment

Thanks

Chapter 29

I woke up next to Zayn but a petit body was between us, Maya was curled up around Zayn. She looked so cute and Zayn was hugging her back, I really wish this was my family. I really wish I could tell Zayn all the truth. "If only you knew." I mumbled between my breath.

I walked to my bathroom and did my daily routine.

While I was brushing my teeth, "Mummy.." I heard Maya whine. "Yes, princess?" I replied, spiting the tooth paste in the white sink. "I don't feel well." She said holding her stomach. "What's wrong, princess?" I asked worriedly. "My tummy." She says pointing to it.

"Are you hungry, babygirl?" She shook her head no. "Okay, how about you hop in bed?" I said and Maya nodded slowly. "Hey, Zayn." I shook him, softly and he opened his breathtaking caramel eyes.

"Yes?" He answered in a deep morning voice. "Good morning, I'm sorry; I woke you up from your beauty sleep but you have to get up." I rolled my eyes.

"Two more minutes." He whined and turned around to face the wall. "Zayn! Get up now what if someone comes in?" I whisper/yelled. "Fine! Fine!" He said annoyed as he got up. "God, What time is it?" He yawns.

"8 AM." I reply. "What?" Zayn screams. I rolled my eyes.

"Mummy!" Maya whimpers, pulling my sweats. "Yes, babygirl?" I place a hand on her forehead. I'll see if she has a high temperature. "My tummy hurts more now." she said as little tears flowed down her face. Her forehead was normal.

"Babygirl, don't cry please." I hugged her. "Wanna go with mummy to make breakfast?" I said to her and she nodded trying to smile but couldn't, it broke my heart into thousands pieces.

"Come on." I said as I picked her up, placing her on my hip and walked down stairs. On my way down, I saw Louis. "Good morning!" Louis said "Morning!" I replied. "Wasn't taking to you; I was talking to Maya!" He stuck out his tongue at me.

"My tummy hurts." She sniffs her pink nose. "What's wrong?" He asked looking over to me, in a more serious tone now. "I don't know this never happened before." I told him. "Need any help?" Louis offered, "No, thanks." I shook my head and walked down to the kitchen, I placed Maya on the counter.

I started making pancakes for all of us and I placed them on the dinning table, "Boys! Breakfast is ready!" I yelled. "C'mon, princess let's go and eat." I said as I sat down on the table with Maya on my lap and then Zayn walked in with a huge smirk oh his face and then the boys entered and started digging in the freshly made pancakes.

After we were all finished, I was cleaned dinning table with Maya still on my hip and Harry helped me. "So how is your tummy, grumpy?" I asked.

"Better but still hurts a wittw." Maya mumbled. "Don't worry princess." I said and she smiled. "Hopefully, it will go away." I reassure her.

I was in my room reading a novel, I was in a grey sweatpants and a golden yellow tank top. I was also wearing my cat eye brown glasses. I actually need them but I wear lenses instead. And my hair was made into a high messy bun; I looked like a total nerd, or geek as Louis prefers to say.

Maya stopped whining about her stomach and now, she is playing on the Xbox with Niall. Suddenly, there was a knock on the door, "Come in!" I yell.

Then Zayn's head pops in, "Hi!" He grinned. "Hey!" I reply not lifting my eyes from my novel. "I have never seen you with glasses before." He analyzed me "You look strange." He concluded.

"You mean ugly strange?" I asked worrildy "Beautiful strange." He said. I was surprised by what he said and also speechless, "T-thank you-u." I stuttered. "You're welcome, my nerdish babe." He smashed his lips to mine and his tongue was down my throat. I kissed him back. I guess I have a little thing for Zayn, or actually a big thing for Zayn. I moved my hands in his hair. "I love you." I mumbled it got out by mistake.

'God! Why did I have to ruin the moment?!' I can feel my cheeks burning from the embarrassment.

"I love you too." He said as he started kissing my neck softly while leaving a love bite every time he could.

'I really hope that doesn't leave a bruise.'

"Hey, we better stop before anyone sees us." I kiss Zayn one last time. "Okay." He kissed me once more and put on his shirt back on, sadly. I put on mine as well.

"You know what?"

"What?" I ask.

"Us breaking up was the worst thing that happened ever to me." Zayn says sincerely.

"Y-yeah." I said in a low voice

"Mariam? Is Zayn here with you?" Liam called entering. "Yes." I answered. "Also Liam have you ever heard of knocking?" I sassed.

"What is Zayn doing here anyway?" He asked looking at him. "Zayn was borrowing a book." I lied. "I was?" Zayn asks. I step on his foot, "I was-Yes, I was." He covers up. "Okay.." Liam says in an awkward tone. "Anyways, Zayn it's football night! Aren't you coming?" Liam said obliviously. "Shit! I totally forgot, mate." Zayn palmed his face. "Zayn, you never forget football night!" Liam said over dramatically. I rolled my eyes at him.

"Let's go!" Liam shouted and headed both Zayn and Liam out of my room. We walked down and Niall was sleeping on the couch with Maya on him "Awe!" We all chorused.

Chapter 30

I was sleeping when I heard a noise. I walked over to the door and looked for where the noise came from, and I opened the door and appeared Zayn smiling mischievously. "Good morning." He said. "What time is it?" I yawn. "6:00 AM." He said calmly. "6:00AM!?" I screamed as he placed his hand on my mouth. "Shh! You're gonna wake up everyone!" He hissed annoyed.

"Zayn, we can't make out." I say. "Why?" he whined. "Why?? Because we are all over this you know it! It never worked out before and won't do anything but make things awkward again! Please, Zayn. I really don't wanna know how will Harry react to this." I say. "But you said you loved me!?" He said looking heart broken."I-I do, but-t it's not like that it's more complicated than that." I sighed sadly.

"Mariam, if you love me and I love you then this will work out please just-" I cut him off. "Zayn, no, I can't do this again, nor to you, nor to Harry, nor to myself." I beg him as tear fell down my face. "Fine." He sighed, his eyes were glassy and his tone was broken and with that he walked away to his room "Zayn," I say in a low voice.

But he never looked back. "I am sorry." I mumbled and with that I walk back to my room a tear ran down my cheek "Mummy, why are you crying?" Maya asks me. "Mummy! Did I do something wrong? "Maya starts tearing up as well. She hugged my leg "Mama, I love you please don't cry." she hugged my legs tightly and I lifted her up. "C'mon, princess let's go back to sleep." I say. "But I'm not sleepy." she whines. "You are, you can barely keep your eyes open." I say as I place her on the bed and she is already asleep.

But as for me I couldn't stop thinking about what I just said why did I ever say that. 'It never worked out in the first place; cause I was pregnant but now I'm not.'.

And we were kids back then, now I'm grown and so as he.

So it could have worked! 'Why did I just have to open my stupid mouth?'

Another tear fell from my eye. I wiped my tears away and wore my glasses and turned on my bedside lamp and grabbed my novel that I was reading before, I was still in the twenty first chapter and it was so interesting.

I kept reading until there was other knock on my door. "Good morning" Niall greeted. "Morning." He responses. "What time is it?" I ask "It's 10:00 AM." Niall answers me. "The look on your face, tells me you haven't slept for even one second, right?" Niall giggled.

"Actually, I did until some thing woke me up so I have been up since 6:00 AM." I say. "6:00 AM! Wow what a coincidence?" Niall says surprised. "What, you too?" I ask. "No, when I went to wake up Zayn he told he was up since 6:00 also." He said. "Wow." I say. "I'll wake up Maya, and head down, Kay?" I said. "Okay, bye then." Niall said and walked out of my room. "Babygirl, wake up now!" I say as she squirms around. "Here comes the tickling monster!" I warn as I tickel her and hear her lovely giggles.

When I walk down with Maya on my hip, "Zii!" She yelled which makes my face flushed red as he looks over to me. He heads over to me and

Maya "Good morning, Maya." He smiles. "Oh and you too." He said never looking over at me and I raised an eyebrow at him.

I wanted to tell him, 'What you're doing is so childish.' Then Maya jumped at Zayn, he took her from me and walked away.

And with that I walk away too I don't have time for this. "Morning, Mariam." Harry smiles at me. "Morning." I smile back. "Hey, I want to tell you, we have an interview today." Harry told me. "Okay, good luck." I say and walk over to the living room where Niall was eating a bag of potato chips and Louis was doing what ever he is doing on his mobile so I opened the T.V and kept changing until I found 'The hunger games: catching fire.'

I love it so kept watching the T.V until Zayn came with Maya on his hip "Mummy!" Maya screamed playing and I walked over to her, she jumped on me and placed her on my lap.

"Mummy, I wanna play?" She begs. "Okay let's go up and get your dolls." I say heading upstairs, me and Maya play for what seemed forever. There was a knock on my door, Zayn appeared. "Harry wanted me to tell that we're going to the interview now." Zayn said to me, like he was a robot and closed the door behind him.

I got up, "Hey Maya, Mummy is gonna go watch T.V, wanna come with?" I ask but she shook her head. "I want to play." She says as she continues to play and I head down to the living room and start watching but then the door bell rang.

I walked over to open the door. I opened it, and saw, "Justin-n.." I stutter shocked. I felt the air leave me lungs, I couldn't breathe.

"You didn't really think I'll never find you, did you?" He grinned. God, I was so scared but not that he'll beat me but that he might hurt Maya. "What-t do y-you want-t from m-me?" I try to make proper sentences but fail. "You are about to know." He smirked again as he throws the door close.

....

Please vote and comment

Thanks

Chapter 31

I n a blur, he slammed his lips into mine and kept kissing me but I backed away and slapped him, it made him really angry.

'Shouldn't have done that!'

He punched me in my face and I fell and my body hit the cold ground but worst of all, my arm was hurting me like hell cause I fell on it "Justin-n, please don't." I beg him but He didn't listen and he kicked my stomach over and over again. I was about to pass out. I felt the air dry out from my lungs.

"Mummy!" Maya cried. At this moment appeared a huge smirk on Justin's face. "Justin-n, n-no I beg-g you please-e s-stay away-y from-m Maya." I beg him holding his leg but he kicked me aside and started looking for Maya. "Maya! Go hide, Now!" I scream at the top of my lungs. and then I hear footsteps getting faster and further.

"You bitch! Shut the fuck up!" He screams at me. "Please don't hurt Maya, you can kill me but don't hurt her. I beg you." I cry. I couldn't move Justin was terribly strong, I could never be even half his strength. "You took away what I wanted and right now, I'm just returning a favor." He grinned and then disappeared, running up stairs, looking for Maya and then I gather some strength and crawl to my phone and I clicked the first contact that came, which was Zayn.

Ringing Ringing Ringing "Zayn, Pick up! Pick up!" I mumble in a very low voice.

"Hello." Zayn says, emotionless.

"Zayn, I-I need you to come right now p-please." I cry through the phone.

"I am on my way, what happened?" He asked in a worried tone.

"Justin, he came here and he is so angry, I can't move at all and now, he is looking for Maya." I cry the last part.

"Hold on, I am coming right now." He says deadly serious

He hangs up.

I was bleeding from my head I guess my head hit the wall when I fell. "Ahh!" I heard a scream from upstairs and then Justin came back with Maya dragging her from her bicep. "Stop! Please leave her." I cry and he throws her on the floor. "Maya!" I cry. My heart has been torn into a billon pieces. I'm the worst mother; I can't save my own daughter.

Justin disappeared again when I looked at Maya she wasn't moving, "Maya." I cry. "Babygirl, please answer mummy!" I cry and then Justin came back with a knife in his hand "Now, I am going to end your useless life." He said simply he walked towards me, when out of the blue Zayn bursts the door open and he starts throwing punches at Justin everywhere but Justin threw the knife on the floor and took a hold of Zayn's neck. Justin was choking him until I crawled to the knife which Justin tired to kill me with and I cut his leg and he falls.

"That's it! Enough games!" He says gritting through his teeth and pulls out of his back pocket, a gun and he heads it towards me but before he could shoot me, Zayn hits his hand and the gun flies all the way across the room and then Zayn keeps throwing punches and kicks to him until he is unconscious.

And I felt a major pain in my side so I look at it and I realize that I'm bleeding from my side where I had a surgery before. "Zayn, call nine-one-one." I say to him. "Please check on Maya!" I beg him "What about you your bleeding?" He says looking at my wounds. "Go check on Maya right now!" I try to scream But it comes out very low Zayn runs to Maya's aid and places his fingers on her neck "Her heart is beating and she is still breathing, must have hit her head." He tells me. "When will the ambulance be here?" I ask in pain. "Very soon." Zayn replied bitting his bottom lip.

Every moment that passed was becoming harder for me to stay awake. I took a peak on my wound and god, I wish I didn't; my shirt was technically red from all the blood and the pain was killing me alive. After what seemed forever I started to close my eyes. I just thought maybe I could rest for a couple of minutes but before my eyelids touch Zayn speaks, "Mariam? Are you awake?" He asks.

Honestly, I really I wanted to answer back but it felt so hard at the moment. All I wanted was to rest my eyes for just a little bit. "I-I am-" before I could finish my sentence, everything turned pitch black and I couldn't see a thing.

I don't want to die just for one reason; just to make sure that Maya is okay and now I know she is alive, so I really won't mind at all, but it's just seeing Maya in all the pain, I never want to her go thought what I went through, I never want that to happen to her specially because of me.

*

*

I hear a lot of beeping sounds next to me and I can feel that my body is on fluffy bed but I can't open my eyes at all; they are too heavy and there is still a major pain in my side so as my head.

'Please, god help me wake up!' I pray in my mind.

I don't wanna leave Maya alone please! She doesn't even know her father!

....

Please vote and comment

Thanks

Chapter 32

I wasn't able to open my eyes still. "Doctor! Is she okay?" I heard some-one ask. "Listen Mr.Malik, she has a fractured arm and there was a huge cut on her head, a enormous bruise on her stomach and her old surgery reopened again." He sighed. "We will be very luck if she can open her eyes." I hear the doctor say.

Zayn's POV:

Mariam was dying in front of my eyes after the doctor told me what she is going through, I walk towards her and sat on a chair next to her bed and I held her hand. "I am so sorry for everything that I have done, but I love you there I said it I love you so damn much, you are the most beautiful person I have ever known. I want to confess something to you, I-I always felt jealous of Maya's father, I don't know who he is but I know he is the luckies man on earth to have you as his girlfriend and Maya as his daughter, but I also know that he is very stupid that he ever left you." I cry

"I wish you were mine, I promise I'll treat you just like the queen, you deserve. I'll get you anything you want." I sigh, "But you're not mine so I guess, so could you stay alive so we could be just friends." I cried and then I felt her hand squeezing mine "Doctor!!" I screamed as he came in as fast as he could. "Doctor, she just squeezed my hand." I explain "This is a good sign. Now sir, you must leave." He told me and I nodded and showed myself out.

I walk to the waiting room and see Harry, Louis, Liam and Niall with sad faces. "How is Maya?" I ask Harry "Well she is okay and she is playing with us but her stomach is bruised terribly." Harry says almost crying but I won't judge him it's his niece and his sister.

"What about Mariam, how is she?" He asked crying his eyes out. "S-she is fine, maybe a little bit below fine but she moved and the doctor told me it's a good thing." I say. "Hey, do you know anything about the guy who did this?" Harry asked me. "No, I don't-" I cut myself, I let out a breath, I didn't know I was holding for so long, then decided to tell the truth, "Yes, I do, but I think Mariam would prefer if she told you the story, herself." I say looking to the room's white tiles.

"Zayn, don't mess with me! Tell me who is this dick who almost killed my sister and niece?" Harry boomed at me and then he looked totally shocked. "I-Is he Maya's father?" Harry asked and horror surrounded his voice. "I don't know." I say looking away. "I am going to go see Maya." I get up and walk over to her room.

Mariam's POV:

Zayn said he was jealous of Maya's father, which is him, I really want to tell him but I don't know how to tell him and what if he didn't want to be Maya's father and even if he did he'd probably hate me cause I hid it on him for almost four years and this is the fifth, but I must tell him and now of course now I owe everybody a explanation about Justin.

After some time about revising my whole life, I open my eyes and saw Harry next to me but, he's crying! "H-Harry?" I stutter. "Mariam!" He says, happiness filling his eyes.

He jumped and hugged me. "I was so worried about you!" He whispered in my ear. "You are the best brother, Harry." I tell him "How is Maya?" I ask him worried "Don't worry about Maya, she is totally fine, she just has a tiny bruise in her stomach but she is her room playing with her dolls, that Niall brought her, so don't worry at all." He calms me down. "Thank you Harry so much for taking care of Maya." I say. "I am doing my job as an uncle." He side hugged me. "And I can assure you, you are the best!" I say, trying to smile.

"Mariam, there is something I'm dying to know and I promise I won't do anything stupid but please tell me, is Justin Maya's father?" Harry asks. "No, what feeling-less father-r a-abuses his-s daughter-r?" I slow down as I just realized what dad used to do to me and my eyes were a little glassier than usual.

Harry understood everything by just the look. "You know what, I bet Shawn was just sick or he was drunk he never knew what was he even saying, but remember he died for you to live." Harry told me. "Thank you, Harry for being here for me." I hugged him. "You're welcome little sis." He whispered.

"By the way, we are going home tomorrow since you woke up today." Harry smiled. "Okay." I say and then he walks out of my room and closes the door behind him. "I have a great brother." I smile. "I hope Harry stays beside me".

....

Please vote and comment ❤

Thanks

Chapter 33

I was home finally, Maya is sleeping while I am sitting in the living room and I am about to explain to the boys about the whole Justin thing. You can imagine how excited I am, note the sarcasm.

"So...." Liam says trying to break the awkward silence.

"Well it all started when I dated him, he treated me perfectly until one day he..." I kept explaining to them. "So what the fuck did he want from you now anyway?" Louis asked "Well I am not really sure but I guess he came here to take revenge.." I answer, unsure.

"How did he even get your address?" Niall wondered. "And how did he know when you were alone in the house?" Harry asked. "I-I don't really know.." I murmured.

"He is dangerous! He must have been watching us to know all of this!" Zayn announced angrily.

After I was done explaining and answering all the boys questions, Zayn suggested that we watch a movie to try to lighten up my mood a bit.

I was cuddling into Zayn, actually we were all sitting next to each other but me and Zayn where a little bit closer to each other, his hand was on my waist and I placed my hands on his.

"By the way, I heard you in the hospital when you said you loved me." I whispered in his ear as I smiled as his face flushed red. "I love you too." I kissed his lips fast before anyone else noticed and then I rested my head on his muscular chest. "I don't love you." He whispers seductively in my ears."I'm obsessed with you." me snuggles closer to me.

After the movie ends, Liam's gets up, "I am going to bed." He announces.

"Goodnight." Louis says as gets up also, "I am going to sleep too." Niall said. "Yeah, me too." Harry completed.

"What about the both of you?" Harry asks us. "No, I'm not sleepy, so I might watch another movie." I say. "Yeah, I'll join her." Zayn backed me up.

We just sat there, enjoying each other's company, we never actually put on an another movie nor did we, do anything. We ended up just sitting there, enjoying the silence and the other's presence. I guess that's what we needed, simply silence and peace.

"Mariam, will you give us another chance cause I don't really know what to call this we are not actually a couple but we act like an actual couple." Zayn explains his point of view which was 100% right.

"I guess we could give it another try." I smile.

"Mariam?" Zayn calls. "Yeah?"

"Will you go on a date with me tomorrow?" He smiles. "I-I-" I didn't expect this, I don't know if I'm ready to go through another relationship again. "It's okay if you don't want to."

"It's not that I don't want to, Zayn. In fact there is nothing I'd love more, it's just I have been through enough wrecks of a relationship, that I can't help but think that this one will just not work one way or another and I don't want to lose you Zayn."

"I don't think I'll ever be okay with losing you for another time."

"Mariam, I desperately understand what you mean, and it's totally normal to think like this after everything you've been through, but this time is different; we're much much older, wiser and we know better; we are not the same kids in high school."

I walked closer to him and sat in his embrace. "Let's go on a date."

I slowly got into bed and hugged Maya closer to me. "How is my baby princess?" I whisper to her sleeping body and she turns to cuddle my hand as I pull her closer to me.

And then I decided I am going to go out with Zayn tomorrow and when we come back from the date I'll tell him the whole truth.

....

Ramdan kareem everyone :)

Chapter 34

I woke up and walked to the bathroom, I did my daily routine and after I was done, I walked up to Maya, "Princess, c'mon wakey wakey." I tickle her she opens one eye. "Mummy, I wanna go to sweep." She whines. "No, wake up now." I say placing her on my hip and we walked down stairs, to the kitchen to see the breakfast made, which was pancakes, and placed on the table. I place Maya on her chair and hear whistling.

I walk to where the whistles are coming from and then I see Zayn in his sweat pants only. I slowly walk to him and cover his eyes "Guess who?" But he didn't answer, he turned around and kissed me and I kissed him back. "Morning, babe." He said in deep morning voice. They way he says 'babe' paralyzes me, it makes my legs so weak.

"Morning, love." I answered then he backed away and flipped the pancake in the pan.

After a few minutes, Zayn was done and we all were eating our delicious pancakes and Maya's face was covered in chocolate syrup as usual, this happens every single time she eats pancake. She looked so adorable.

Soon we all finished and by we I meant by the whole crew. And this time I wasn't cleaning, Louis and Niall were, it was their turn. 'Hahahaha!' laughs evily internally so no one think I am crazy, I just really really hate doing the dishes and cleaning up after we eat.

So right now, I am sitting on the couch in the living room, checking my facebook. Maya is playing with her toys in front of me, on the floor. Zayn is in his room.

This is what a normal life looks like.

I wanted to watch some movies on Netflix so as I head up stairs to bring my headphones.

So as I was walking through the hallway to my room, "BOO!!" Zayn pops in front of me "AAAHHH!!" I scream "Oww, my ears hurts, thanks to you, now." He winces. "Well, I am not the one, who tried to scare the HELL out of you." I say in a duh tone. "So.. Since you are not doing anything and neither am I, so why don't we go out a little." Zayn smirks.

"Well...-" I was cut off by Zayn "I didn't really mean for you to answer that, I AM taking you out whether you like it or not." He says like it's the most obvious thing in the world. "Wha-" He cut me off again. "Go get dressed, now!" He says and goes back to his room.

I walk to my room to go and get dressed, I throw on blue jeans and a white pullover and white converse and I grab my nude colored bag. I head to Zayn's room, I knock on his door. "Hi." I smile as he opened the door. "Wow!" He says checking me out "Impressed?" I grin "Very." He says. He was in blue ripped jeans as well and blue shirt that said 'Not now.....Maybe tomorrow' and dark blue converse.

"You don't look so bad yourself." I say as he grins as we walk down stairs. "Where are you two going?" Harry asks "For a walk." Zayn says. I took a couple of seconds but then I decided to go with Zayn's plan but I really wanted to tell Harry the truth. "Yeah, Harry, could you watch Maya for me?" I say. "Okay." Harry smiles and then we both go head to the door and get out.

'I really hate lying to Harry; it gives me these guilt knots in my stomach.'

Harry's POV:

'There is definitely something going with them.'

'I just hope nothing happened between them again cause last time Mariam, traveled and Zayn, shut everybody for almost a year.' I sigh.

'They seem so happy together.' I smile internally.

"HARRY, COME IT'S YOUR TURN WITH NIALL!" Liam screams.

"COMING!" I yell back.

'I am going to beat Niall's ass, I will totally win'.

Zayn's POV:

I don't even know how this happened, all I know that it happened so fast and now I am on a date again with Mariam, Just like the old days and even better, "So where are we going?" She asks looking to me. "You will see when we get there, now get in the car." I say opening her door for her as she gets in.

I walk over to the driver's seat and start the car. She turned on the music and started singing 'Wouldn't Be Love' by R I T U A L.

She had an amazing voice. And then 'All Of Me' by John legend so it got into me and I started humming, until I ended up singing and Mariam was staring at me. "Did I say something wrong?" I asked "No, it's just you have beautiful voice." She smiles "Well, I am 'the Zayn Malik." I smirk.

Mariam's POV:

Zayn, suddenly stopped the car we were in front of a park. I got out so as he, "Zayn, please tell me where are you taking me?" I ask entering the Park. "This park was where me and the guys used to hangout and rehearsal, and some times I used to come here on my own when I needed space, this place is so special to me, and you are the only I showed this place too. I mean now, me, you and the guys know about this place." He half smiles at the end. "Wow!" I mouth.

It was really huge, full of trees and flowers. "Oh my god, this place looks so magical!" I say. I was a huge fan of nature. I can stare aimlessly at the sky for hours and watch as her beautiful colors dance in front of me.

"I know, this place is where very important events happened and today will happen one also." Zayn told me.

I was so overwhelmed with the beautiful trees, plants and flowers. The whole view was breathtaking. When I turned back to look at Zayn, he was on one knee.

He got out a ring, "Mariam, I love you, I love you more than I love anything in my whole life, Will you marry me?"

I was so speechless. I tried to speak but no words got out of mouth. "I-I-" I wasn't able to form words. Zayn's eyes looked nervous. I didn't know what to do. I took a deep breath and let it out, then I answered him.

Chapter 35

Z ayn got up and kissed me, "I'm going to make a sandwich, want anything?" Zayn asks me. "No, thank you." I blow him a kiss.

I was still reading 'Everything, Everything' I was almost finished with it.

Then flashbacks come from the day Zayn proposed. "Will you marry me?" He asks. "Zayn, I really appreciate that you showed me to this dazzling park, but don't you think we moving a bit too fast?"

He gets up from his position he looked like he was about to cry, but never did. "Zayn, please stop." I hug him. "I love you more than anything in my whole life but I don't wanna move fast so we don't regret it in the future. I'm doing this because I care about our future." I cupped his cheeks in my hand.

After I say this Zayn hugs me back. "I love you, more." Zayn kisses my forehead. "I can't afford to lose you again." He whispers into my hair. "Neither can I." I hold on to him, tighter.

"Wanna go eat some where? I don't wanna go home now, do you?" Zayn offers. I shake my head. "Let's go." I kiss his lips and hold his hand while walking out.

And that's it, that what exactly happen at the park. Zayn and I are dating like nothing happened.

Zayn came back with a delicious, looking sandwich. I snatch it quickly and take a big bite. "Hey!" Zayn whines. "I asked you if you want anything." Zayn pouts. "I know but where is the fun in that. "Fine, have it the way you want but I will take revenge." He says as he jumps on me and starts tickling me. "God! Zayn stop! I'm ticklish." I say as I tear up from laughing too hard.

"Zayn!" I scream but he never stops. "Please-I can't breathe." I am out of breath from all the laughing. "Will you stop eating my food?" He asks and I nod defeated. "Good." He smirks, in victory. I roll my eyes.

"So how is Maya doing, isn't she going to school tomorrow?" He asks. "Oh please don't remind me." I roll my eye. "She hates school so much, like they torture her!"

"You should see what's bothering her maybe she is dealing with some thing serious." Zayn suggests, taking a bite from his sandwich.

"I asked her a million times if something or someone is bothering her but she keeps saying no. What do I do?"

"Maybe I can talk to her?" He says. "Okay, go ahead but why would she hide a thing like this from me, her mom and tell you?" I raise an eyebrow.

"Because, I'm the funny and cute uncle 'Zii'!" He say it as Maya does, which is in a high squeaky voice and I laugh.

"Fine, you can try." I half smile.

"Okay, goodnight."

"Hey! You're too early! Am I supposed to sit here alone?! Everyone is sleeping." I pout.

"Exactly, so you should sleep too and 3:00 AM is not early." Zayn smirks.

"Goodnight." I get up to kiss him and then both of us head to out rooms. I walk towards my bed and climb beside Maya. I kiss her forehead and the drift into sleep.

*

*

I wake up and shake Maya, slowly. "Mommy, I'm sick, and I can't go to school today." She whines. "Oh is that so? Because we have bubble gum ice cream and I would have given you some but since you're sick then I can't. I guess I'll have to eat it all by myself." I fake a sad face. "Bubble gum ice cream?" Maya screams as her eyes got wider. "Yup, but you can only have it after school." I tell Maya. "C'mon, let's get you dressed." I say.

After I dressed Maya in a blue skirt with a yellow flower, a baby pink t-shirt and tiny adidas sneakers, that fit her feet perfectly. I combed her beautiful golden brown hair and left it loose, but I added a yellow hair band.

"Ice cream now?" She asks. I shake my head, "After school."

She looks down as if I destroyed her dream. "Does grumpy want breakfast?" I as lifting her up, and placing her on my hip. She shakes her head sadly.

"But then strawberry shortcake is gonna be sad you didn't eat her delicious strawberries."

"Strawberries?" She waves her eyebrows and I laugh.

*

*

I sent Maya to school and then I drove back home the boys have new interview, hope this one works out not like the other one which I ruined for them. Then my phone started ringing.

"Hello?" I answer. "Hey babe!" Zayn's voice makes me smile automatically. "How did the interview go?" I ask. "Not good." He answers, sadly. "Oh, I'm sorry, Zayn but there will-" I was cut off by him. "Kidding! We totally nailed it and we're going on tour next week!" Zayn breaks the new. "Yay! I'm so, so happy for you." I smile.

Harry knows about Zayn and I being together but he's still a bit uncomfortable.

*

*

Time passed, Zayn was still 'just signing papers' and I have to pick Maya up right now.

I got dressed, actually just threw on whatever I saw first, grabbed my phone and my bag then head to my car. While I was on the way my phone started ringing, "Hello?" I picked up. This time there was no answer, "Anyone there?" I ask. Then the other line goes dead. 'Must be wrong number but still rude.'

I parked my car and got out. I started looking for Maya, and it was strange because she wasn't at her same spot.

I see that most people have gone home. I was staring to get worried. I walked into the school, I asked the security guard about her, "Oh, I have seen this girl!" He says pointing to mobile, as I'm showing a picture of Maya. "Where is she?" I say louder than I thought. "She left with her father? I think so." He says unsure. "Father?" I choke. "Yes, ma'am." I nodded back at him.

I walked away and started started dialing Zayn's number.

'Maybe Zayn is late because he picked up Maya to surprise me. But why will he do this without telling me?'

My hands were shaking badly while I was dialing in his number. "Hello, babe? How is everything?" Zayn answers.

"Zayn, Is Maya with you?" I feel my heart go faster. Honestly, I didn't want him to answer that question. "No, why? Aren't you picking her up?" Zayn throws at me a couple of questions. I started sobbing to the phone. I walked inside my car and sat there. My hands were now shaking terribly. "Mariam, Mariam! Calm down please and tell me what happened?"

"Zayn, I can't find Maya-I asked the security guard-d and he told me she went with her father." I lost breath after saying this. "Mariam, calm down before you get sick and try to think about where could she be or who would she have gone with? I'm on my way to the school. Wait for me and Harry there. The other lads are gonna stay at home in case she comes back."

"She won't come back! She is 4 year old who doesn't know how to say 'sandwich'." I yell. "She definitely doesn't know her way home!"

"I'm on my way, just hold on." I nod and hung up.

*

*

I was sitting in the car, tears blurred my vision, my hands were shaking so hard and breathing got harder each second. My phone started ringing, must be Zayn or the other lads. I tried as best as I can to read the ID caller.

It said 'Blocked', but I picked up. "Who-o is this-s?" I try to speak. "Oh, don't tell me you don't remember me?"

I choked on my own tears. "M-Mark?" I lost my breath. "That is a right guess!" He yells. I was about to hang up when, "Don't hang up, I know where your little 'Maya' is?" I stopped dead in my tracks, right now I had two choices, either to start yelling and cussing at him, or beg him for more information.

I chose the first option. "Mark, you son of a bitch, if you don't tell where my daughter is, I will burry you alive! Can you hear me?!" I scream with all anger filling me. "If I were you, I would keep my mouth shut, especially when someone is helping you." He said annoyed as if I offended him.

I couldn't breathe at all. I wanted to die in this car seat, I wished it could swallow me alive right now. "First, we gotta set off some rules." I could sence his stupid smirk through the phone. "O-okay." I mange to get out. "Good."

....

Please vote and comment ♥

Thanks

Chapter 36

"Yes, douche." I scream to the phone. "I said drop that attitude." He gritted through the phone.

I rolled my eyes, letting go of a breath, I was holding for too long.

"Take the next U-turn, then turn right, you'll see a mini market there, park your car there." Mark guides me to where ever he's leading me to.

"Mark! Why are you doing this? Why are you even helping me?" I ask as soon as I realize he's helping me.

"Because-" He sighs. "She's with Justin and I don't trust him, he can hurt her badly." Mark confesses. "She's with who?! Justin!!" I can't help but start sobbing again.

I was so confused, I didn't know what to do at all! I was so helpless. I felt so guilty for not telling Harry and Zayn, where am I, they are probably on their way to the school, to see that I'm no where to be found and they'll get really worried but that was the deal, Mark and I made, I can't tell anyone about this and he'll help me find Maya.

"Stop crying, please. We'll get her back."

I wanted to ask him a lot of questions like, 'How did he know about Justin?, How did he know Maya's place? And why didn't want me to tell anyone if he is really helping me?'

"Look Mark, there is alot of things which I don't know about, like how do you know Justin took Maya, but I am willing to trust you, so please Mark, put anything that I did to you aside. This is a 4 year-old child, who didn't do one single wrong thing in her life and she is kidnapped because of me." I spill.

"Don't worry, Mariam; I really want to help you." He replies.

"I'm there." I whisper through the phone. "Okay, get out of the car and I will find you." Mark commanded me. "Okay."

As soon as I hung up, my phone boomed with my ringtone breaking the quietness around me. The caller ID read 'Zaynie' But I declined. Then my phone blew up with messages from Zayn, Harry, Louis, Niall and Liam.

'Mariam!! Where are you?? Pls answer me I am going to have a heart attack' I read one of the messages. "I'm so sorry, Zayn." I whisper.

When I turned around I was welcomed with Mark almost only 2 inches apart.

"There, I found you." He smiled. "Mark," I breathe out. "Don't sneak up on me like that."

"Sorry." He whispers.

"C'mon follow me." He says grabing my hand. "Where are we going?" I ask.

"To where I've been hiding." He tells me. "What?" I stand there not understanding. "I've been crashing here since I got no where to go." He mumbles. "Ohh." Was all I could get out of my system.

After he made me follow him into a lot of hallways, we ended up in a ugly room which reeked by the way.

"Mark, I'm sorry but what are we doing here?"

Mark turned around but he looked different, he had a guilt look on his face, as if he murdered someone. "Mark?"

"I'm sorry but I can't back down now." He told me.

"What are-" I was cut off by a powerful punch being thrown to my face. I blacked out at once.

*

*

"Wakey waky sleepy head." Someone said, his voice was familiar. I couldn't still see well, all I could make out was his silhouette. "Mark! You liar! You son of b-" I started screaming.

"I'm not Mark! Open your damn eyes!" The silhouette ordered. I blinked a couple of times then I saw him! It was Justin. "Justin?" I asked in horror. I tried to get up from this filthy chair, but little did I know, I was actually tied to it. "Where is Maya? I swear if you touch one hair of her's, I will rip your heart out and shove it so far down your throat." I scream.

He just laughs. "That's the cutest threat I ever gotten." He laughs again.

Suddenly, his facial expression changed. "Your precious daughter is here with me." He shouts. "And you will see her." He said smirking again.

"But there is one condition, babe."

"Don't call me babe you asshole, give me my daughter!!"

"You fucking don't know how serious this is!" He shout loudly.

"The condition is you simply have to marry me." He grins.

"What? No, never! Over my dead body." But I earned a slap.

It stung me so badly. A tear which was not meant to fall ended up rolling down my cheek. "Trust me, I tried to maintain myself and do this the easy way but you just have to be a bitch, don't you?"

"This is not an option Mariam! You either marry me and get Maya back or I swear you'll never see Maya again, understand?" He grabs my neck so hard. I couldn't help but cry.

"Justin please just give me back Maya and I swear I won't tell a single soul about this just please let me see Maya." I sob.

"Are you crazy?" He mocks. "Do you think you'll just get what you want?" He raises his eyebrow.

"Choose one of the options I gave you, but I have to tell you if you choose not to marry me, I'll still keep you here, because I can't just let you out, can I?" He laughs.

"I need an answer, bitch!" Another slap was sent to my right cheek. "Uggh." I grunt from the impact. My hands and body were visibly shaking now.

I had a terrible headache. Everything was getting blurry and I felt so week. I could hear my heart pounding inside my chest "Mariam?" I could hear Justin's voice starting to fade. "Mark!" I heard him shout as I started to lose consciousness. "Mark!!!" He shouts louder. That was the last thing I could remember before everything turned pitch black.

*

*

"What's wrong with her, Doctor?" I heard Mark ask. "Well everything seems to be okay right now, maybe she just over exerted herself. Make sure she her vitals are okay." The Doctor replied.

I opened my eyes, weakly. "Thanks doc. Sure will." Mark nodded and with that the doctor walked out. I know I could have just called for the doctor and tell him I'm kidnapped but I couldn't speak. I don't know what happened to me. "How are you doing now?" Mark questioned me. "Ahh, please stop screaming!' I cry. "I-I wasn't-" He stutters.

He started with his piercing brown orbs into my weak hazel ones to see if I'm lying or not, but sadly I wasn't.

I realized this time I wasn't tied to old ugly chair, in fact I was lying on a huge king-sized bed.

Mark lets out a sigh, "You're going to see Maya tomorrow, Justin and I agreed on this but you need to give him an answer by tomorrow." He says worriedly as if he has a heart, that backstabbing asshole! He is the whole reason I am here!

"You should rest right now." He says a bit too sternly. "Here take this for your headache." He says handing me a blue pill.

I swallowed it and laid back, resting my head on the white fluffy pillow.

Mark headed out of the room, which I was in, then I heard him talking to someone. "How the fuck are you sure she can't run away, when she is lying on YOUR bed in YOUR room with an unlocked door?!"

"Shh! She might hear you!" Mark screams.

'There is no way for me out of this hell hole, is there?' I ask myself.

The problem is that I couldn't think straight this headache was abnormal it's too strong and it's taking too long to go away, the pain is killing me.

Chapter 37

I was sleeping peacefully when suddenly the headache kicked in again. "Ahh!" I scream, waking up. I limp out of the bed, trying to find anyone to help me. "Justin?" I cry. The headache was getting stronger each second. Tears started rolling down my cheeks from the pain. I did my best and tried to walk. Then somebody appeared. "Mariam? What are you doing here?" Justin asks looking confused. "I have a bad headache." I barely say above whisper.

Then I fell to floor; my feet just couldn't carry me. "Oh My God." Justin said quickly as I fell. He kneeled down next to me. "It hurts.." I whimper. "Shh.. I'm calling the Doctor right now." He informs me.

*

*

"What the fuck are you talking about? You didn't say this will happen!?" Justin yells from the other room. "I didn't say anything! I gave you the drugs you asked for!" I hear the Doctor shout back.

'What?!! Justin has been giving me fake medicine!?'

I tried to stand up but his time one of my wrists was tied to the bed. I tried to untie it with my other one but no luck; it's tightly knotted.

"I see you're up." Justin gives me a fake smile. "Get the hell away from me!" I scream. "Mariam, you're just sick and probably just hallucinating-"

"Did the Doctor say that or did you make that up just like you drugged me."

His fake smile turned at once, "You were eavesdropping, weren't you?"

"First, YOU were shouting and second, YOU'RE FUCKING DRUG-GING ME! And YOU kidnapped my daughter and I, and you're the one to talk?"

"I didn't kidnap you, you came with yourself willingly." He spread his lips into a 6-inch smirk. "I came because I thought I was going to find my daughter!" I shout. "I don't care about your motives; you're here anyways."

"Are you out of your mind?! Justin, if you don't get me Maya, I'll-"

"You'll what? Scream? Shout? Cry? Beg me hopelessly?" He mocked walking closer. When he was close enough I punched his face. "Oww! You bitch!" He screams holding his nose which was bleeding.

"Show me Maya!" I scream. "You wanna see her?" He says letting go of his bleeding nose. "Fine!" He spats.

He walks over to the bed, where my wrist is tied, the only thing that stopped me from punching him again, is that he's making me see Maya, but I just can't trust him.

He untied me, then grabbed my bicep. He dragged me into couple of hallways which I couldn't differentiate between them. His grip did hurt but I kept my mouth shut. Until we were standing in front of a door.

"Be my guest," Justin smiles. I hestiate a little before I opened the door before I opened it. When I did I saw Maya!

She was so pale and had tear stains on her face, but there was a huge purple bruise on her cheek. "Oh my god." My breathing level increased. "Mommy!" she screams crying. "Maya!" I hug her.

"You animal!" I screamed unhugging Maya and walking towards him. "You wanted to see her, well you did. "How could you hurt her again?" I said as I was about to punch him but he caught my hand. "Tell me you didn't just try to hit me," He raised his eyebrow, "Again?" He finishes off. "You shouldn't have done that." He grits through his teeth.

He started to tighten his grip on my hand, and it was starting to get numb. I wanted to cry, scream, do anything to release pain. "You'll pay for it, bitch."

He pushed me backwards, and pinned me to the wall. "Mommy-y?" Maya started to cry. "Justin, please at least don't do this in front of Maya." I couldn't help but cry. "But that's the best part." He whispers in my ear. Justin started to punch me.

One punch comes after it another. With each one, I got weaker. "Stop! Stop!" Maya screams. I slowly slid to the ground. I wasn't able to breathe properly. "Get up!" Justin shouted. "Oh wait you can't." He mocked. "Because you're an ungrateful hoe!" He grabs my neck and hold on it tighyly. "P-please-e s-stop." I beg.

Justin acted like he didn't hear me. He gripped even tighter than before then he threw me on the floor and when I thought this torture ended, he started kicking me.

I could barely open my eyes. I tried to back away but he caught me by my hair. "Please-e, I-I can't take anymore."

"No! No! Leave her alone!" Maya screams pushing him. "Move Maya or I will hurt you!" He threats. "Maya, princess-ss p-please m-move." I cry. "No, mommy." She cries hugging me.

My head started throbing! "Ahh!!" I scream. "Got what you deserve bitch." He rolled his eyes and walked away. "Mommy?" Maya crys. "Mommy?!" She yells louder. "Mommy!!?" She called once more before I blacked out.

*

*

I woke up in a bed again, this time it was a different room. 'Where am I? Where is Maya?!' I thought.

"You're up thank god." Mark says. "Where is Maya?!" I ask. "She's in her room."

I get up without hesitation but the pain of beaten body pulled me back. "You really shouldn't have tried to hit Justin." Mark 'advises' me, note the sarcasm.

I have had it with him. I got up and punched him really hard that my knuckles got bruised a bit. "That's for backstabbing me!" Then another punch flew to his face, "And that's for not stopping Justin when he hurt Maya!" Then one last punch square in his nose. "This one was for every-thing you did in general!"

"How was I so stupid to ever love you?! God, I must have been blind!" I spit in his face.

'Damn! This power felt so good.'

Then I searched for something to knock him out with. 'Think! Think! Think!' I yelled to conscience.

Then I found a bottle on the beside table I grabbed it and I held it high in the air ready to hit him. "M-Mariam! P-please d-don't do this-s.." He says barely able to put words together.

"I'll help you get out!" He shouts.

"Yeah just like you helped me get in!?" I scream.

"Y-you were unconscious when you came here, you won't know your way out, but I will help you." He begs. "Look who's begging whom now." I spat with confidence. "Pl-please, I-I know I was a douche for betraying you like that but I had to-I have a very good reason." He explains himself.

"I don't care about your reasons! You betrayed my trust in something deadly serious and apart from the fact that Maya is my daughter, you stood there while watching him hurt a 4-year old."

"I-I-" He was speechless; what he did was a hundred percent wrong and the asshole knew it.

"You know what I can actually forgive you for betraying me but I can never forgive you for letting Justin lay a finger on Maya." I shout smashing the bottle on his head.

'I gave him a chance and ruined it, right!'

'I hope he is not dead! God, please don't make him die, please.'

Enough about him. I needed to find Maya and get the hell out of here! I tiptoed my way out of the room. I don't know if I was loud that Justin heard or not but I had to be fast anyway. I ran wandering through hallways. I don't where I was going, damn, I didn't even know if I was moving forward or in circles.

"MARK! Where the hell are you?!" I heard Justin shout. Shit that means he's close! I took a deep breath and opened a random room and jumped in. I let out my breath, slowly shaking my head to make the least noise as possible.

"Mark!!!" Justin yelled again. His footsteps were becoming faster and louder, exactly like my heart beats.

I knocked out Mark but the thought of even punching Justin seemed impossible.

Justin was right outside the room I was standing inside. I held tightly to the wall as leaned my back to it. Little did I know there was so what seemed like a stick made of metal which I kicked by mistake and it made a sound which is not loud but you can hear it when you're standing 4 inches apart.

'Shit!! He definitely heard this!'

The door started to open so I jumped behind it. Justin walked in, scanning every inch of the already pitch black room. He walked 3 exact steps forward then stopped. My heart was about to pop out.

Without even thinking twice, I knelt really quite to pick up the metal stick then I jumped from behind the door and got out slamming the door shut behind me and locking it with metal stick. "Mariam!!" Justin shouts at the top of his lungs. "You will pay for this! I can assure that!"

He banged loudly against the wooden door. 'I gotta fucking hurry!'

Well since Justin already knows that I'm out might as well shout! "Maya!! Where are you?" I scream to the void.

"Mum!!" I heard a fade scream. "Maya keep shouting I coming Babygirl!" I scream running as fast as I can. "Mummy! I'm here!" She shouts again.

Her beautiful voice was getting louder. It was like music to my ears.

"Mummy!" She yells again. "I'm almost there princess."

Then I was there standing right in front of her door. I knew it because that was the only room where the lights were on.

"Maya! Mummy's here!" I scream twisting the doorknob. It didn't open.

'No! No! No! Please open!'

"Mummy! What's wrong?" Maya worries.

"Baby, just get back!" I tell her.

I pushed the door once, twice and even thrice then even more. I pushed myself against the strong wooden door so many times I lost count.

"Mummy!" Maya starts to cry. "Princess please don't cry! Everything is going to be okay! Don't worry!"

"Don't tell her that. You wouldn't want lie to your daughter, would you?"

Chapter 38

"Mummy!" Maya starts to cry. "Princess please don't cry! Everything is going to be okay! Don't worry!"

"Don't tell her that. You wouldn't want lie to your daughter, would you?"

He tried to punch me but I ducked. "You thought you could get rid of me so easily?" He smirked.

I threw a punch directed to his nose, which of course he dodged. "Nice one."

But before I knew it he pushed me against the wall. "Maybe you're not that weak after all." He grins.

I squirm around trying to get out of his awfully tight grip. "Let go of me!" I yell trying to push him off of me.

"Mummy? Where are you?" Maya calls. "Mummy is busy right now."

"Indeed she is, Maya. So I suggest you go back to sleep because there is no escaping tonight."

I took this chance and kicked him where the sun doesn't shine. "Ahh! You bitch!" He yells curling up on the floor. Then a key chain fell out of his right pocket. This must be it! I grabbed it and started inserting key by key to the door, until one clicked. I opened the door and Maya came running to me, hugging my legs. "Mummy." She mumbles.

"Baby girl, I need you to run as fast you can! Okay and when you get out of here tell anyone to take you the police station." I whisper.

She nodded, "But Mummy won't come with me?"

"I don't think so."

Justin started to get up, "Run Maya! Run!" I scream as she runs far away.

I block Justin from trying to get her which makes him angry. "Ahh!" He let out a loud scream of frustration. He starts kicking me when he realizes he'll never catch up with Maya. He kicks me, and punches me so hard that I couldn't keep standing.

"You thought you could run away from me?!" He screams. "I'll show you!"

He grabs my bicep and throws my whole body against the cold wall. He kicks my legs too many times that I cannot catch my breath. Slowly, everything fades in a darker shade until pitch black darkness was the only thing I could see.

Maya's POV:

I was lost! I didn't know where to go! I did get out of this filthy place I was in but I don't know how to go to the police station. It was night so no one was around but weird looking people that scared me.

Some guys kept staring at me to I started to skip. The footsteps behind me started to fasten as well. I started to run as fast as my legs could but little did I know there was someone standing in front of me. "Ouch!" I say as I fell."Are you lost?" He asks.

This might be a trick question, cause if I say no then he might ask me where is my mum and if I say yes he will kidnap me!

"I-I-" I couldn't form words.

Then the guy I was running from caught up to me! I jumped. "Is he bothering you?" He asks me, I nodded unsure.

"Dude, She is my little sister and she ran away. I'm trying to take her back home." The one running after me says, or lies.

"Is that true?" I shake my head. "C'mon sissy, don't be a little bitch-"

"She said she is not the one your looking for please get back." The one next to me says.

The other guy moves towards me, but the one I'm standing next to, pulls me behind him. "Leave! Now!" He shouts.

The other guy runs the in opposite direction. But this guy turns and kneels down to me. "Are you lost?" He repeats. I nodded unsure.

"Can you please take me to the police station?" I do as mommy told me to. He smiles then nods, "Sure-" He stops for me to tell him my name. I don't know if I should or not but he helped me so could be like returning a favor.

"Maya."

"Maya, hmm." He repeats, saying it as if he is tasting the magic in the word.

"What a beautiful name!" He replied a little bit late. "Thank you-" I do the same.

"Oh! I'm Robin." He says laughing.

Mariam's POV:

I woke up in the freezing floor. I couldn't move; every part of me hurt! I wanted to get up and figure my way out this hell but every movement hurt like I've been hit by a train.

I try my best to get up, wincing with each movement. The room was dark, dusty and reeked terribly but there was no Justin in here. At first I couldn't see a thing but slowly my eyes adjusted to the darkness.

I crawl forwards, not knowing where I was heading. My left bicep hurt awfully, it must be broken so I shift my weight to my right arm.

I crawl and crawl until a door a appears. I'm pretty sure it's locked but let's try to open it anyway. Very quietly, I twist the door knob and it opens.

'What the hell-Justin must be either really dumb or he is planning something terrible.'

I get up onto my feet, in case I need to run or fight.

I wander through these identical hallways again. Justin was nowhere to be found.

'Something is vastly wrong.' I walk towards some pitch black rooms, peaking inside them, looking for Justin or Mark but there was no trace to the both of them. I started to skip a little bit faster; the more I'm here the more I freaked out I get.

I stopped as soon as I saw a dead end! 'Wtf?!'

There was nothing but olive colored, dirty wall. I ran the opposite way running into the same rooms. After I got to the very last other end I found the same thing, a wall blocking my way out!

'What am I gonna do?' I fall to my knees crying. "I can't get out of this stupid place!" I cry out loud. "I don't even know if I'm in a basement or I'm on ground level." I cry hysterically.

Maybe I should start looking for a map, a phone, anything, that could help me. I headed to the room I was first in.

It was just as I felt it cold, dark and dirty. I started looking around for props. When suddenly a piece of a cut wallpaper in the floor.

This is wallpaper! It must be covering a window or something. I pulled the already half fallen off green wallpaper. Uncovering wall by wall until I got the last wall out of four.

"Please god! please help get out of here." I pray with the last ounce of hope inside me.

I remove the wallpaper, half way through finishing the wall a door appears only one problem it had no knob! How could I possibly open it.

Then I removed my T-shirt and got out a metal stick from my bra. I inserted it inside the door and pushed it and then I pulled the door my way. 'Oh my god! I can't believe what I'm seeing in front of me!'

Chapter 39

I couldn't believe it I-I was outside.. The sun hit my sore skin for the very first time in a while. I started shaking so badly and sobbing heavily. I made it out alive! I just couldn't wrap my head around it. I never thought I was going to see another day.

I don't know how long I have been there but all I know it was too long. I scan my surroundings, I don't know where am I. All I see is a couple of empty parked cars that have a loaded layer of dust resting on them which means they have been here for some good time too and at the not very far, rested a lonely convenience store.

I walked in, "Hello, do you have a phone I could use please?" The guy behind the counter ran towards me. "Ma'am, are you okay?" He asks worriedly. I nod weakly. "Please, may I borrow your phone?" I ask once more.

"Yeah sure!" He says quickly handing me his cell phone. I enter Zayn's number. The phone starts to ring while my hands are still shaking.

"Here!" The guy hands me a juice box and bottle of water, while having a warm smile on his face. He seemed like he was 19 or so but not a year older.

I paused for a second. "Please take them! They are on me." He gives them to. "T-thank you-u.." I mange to blur out. I was so overwhelmed that I forgot the phone ringing in my hand. The call was on going for 0:03 seconds and I was still staring at the screen not believing Zayn picked up.

"Hello? Is anyone there?"

I could hear his voice it seemed sad but god I missed it so much. I missed him so much. Tears race down my cheeks. "Zayn-n.." I cry.

"Oh my god.. Mariam? Is that you?" He screams. "I-I-" I didn't know what to say.

"Are you okay? Mariam! Where are you?!" Zayn explodes with all these questions. "Zayn, I-I am f-fine. But is Maya with you?" I asked him this question and could feel my heart's pace go faster, I feel like there is a lump in throat to speak anymore.

"Yes, yes she is. This 'guy' took her to the police station and they announced about a lost child and we found her."

"Is she okay?" I cry. I don't know why am I crying anymore but I can't help it.

"We took her to the hospital to get her checked, thank god; it was nothing serious, only one bruise on her cheek which is almost gone by now but she is asking for you every second."

"I am fine but I don't know where I am. Wait! Wait!"

"Excuse me..eh Blake-e?" I take a while to read his clipped-on tag. "Yes, ma'am." He answers. "Could you tell me where am I?"

"You are at San Yisdro."

"I am on the outskirts of the United States! At San Yisdro." I inform Zayn.

"I am coming right now! Don't move!" Zayn hangs up.

"Thank you so much for everything, Blake." I whisper to him while handing him back his phone.

"Blake is my last name, I go by Alex." He flashes a small smile at me.

"So erm..can I ask you what happened?" Alex asks shyly.

I took a deep breath then I spoke, "Actually, I have been talking about it for too long can we talk about something else please?"

"Oh-yeah! Sure! I am so sorry if I overstepped a boundary." He apologizes hysterically. I place my hand on his. "Hey, hey. It was an honest mistake; you didn't know and it's fine." I smile.

A good few hours passed and I talked with Alex for sometime. He told me he has two younger siblings, a boy and a girl. His father died when he was really young and his mother is trying to keep a roof over their head so hard. He is working here to save for collage, Yale to be specific and of course, he is doing this to help his mom in the first place.

I thought that was really thoughtful of him. Nowadays, not a lot of teenagers tend to help their parents.

"I am sure she really appreciates what you're doing, Alex."

He looked towards me and nodded. "Hey! There is a black car beeping outside! Is that meant for you?"

I ran so fast, heading towards the car. The car's passenger door opened and Harry came out. I hugged him so hard. Harry took sometime to process all what's happening then he wrapped his shaking arms around me. "Mariam," He whispered in my hair. "I missed you so fucking much." He tighten his grip around my waist.

'Great, the water works is going to start again.' I mentally roll my eyes.

"Harry?" I rest my wounded cheek on his shoulder. "Yes, Mariam." He softly strokes my hair with his warm hand while holding me with the other.

"Don't ever fucking leave me again!"

"I shall die if this happens." I burry my face in his neck just like a small child running to his big brother after the big bad bully kicked his ass at school. I never wanted to let go.

"Mommy?" I was so overwhelmed with my feelings to notice my surroundings. Zayn was standing right next to me, with my maya on his hip.

'She', 'she' is the reason why I have to get my shit together. I can't fall down! I can't break! I can't give up because of her, Maya. My reason for living, my rainbow after the rain and my ray of sunshine at the end of the dark tunnel.

"She wanted to tag along and honestly, no could stop her." Zayn laughed. "Mommy!!" She screamed jumping on me. "M-Maya." I was so shocked. I let out a breath which was in for too long. "Mommy, don't ever let go of me! Mommy! Please stay with me!" She hugs me and lays her head on my chest.

I can't believe it. She just said the same thing I said to Harry. She felt the same thing I felt!

No! No! No! I promised myself I'd never let my daughter feel the same way I felt! I promised I'd never let her go through what I went through but I failed! I failed myself, I failed her, my mother and anyone who ever had hope in me.

"Stop crying mommy! No more bad guy here." She tells me, placing a hand on my shoulder. What can four-year-old ever do to deserve this? Nothing.

A toddler can do fucking anything and still won't deserve to go through this, never know her father, see her mother get beaten in front of her, get kidnapped, punched and kicked.

I failed her in all ways possible. I don't deserve her. I never did, but selfish me, had to keep her. I was too selfish to give her up. I couldn't live knowing she is living with her adoptive mother, telling her everyday that she loves her, calling her mom and giving her hugs and kisses.

A supportive hand rested on my shoulder. There was a warm smile on Zayn's face. He was trying to tell me that I did good, making me feel okay but I didn't deserve that too.

'Get in.' Zayn motioned to the car. I looked back searching for Alex and found him near the counter and mouthed a 'thank you'. He nodded in response, giving me another smile.

The car ride was so quite that nothing could be heard but Maya's soft snores. Zayn was is in the driver's seat while Harry in the passenger's and last but not least I and Maya were at the back with her resting her head in my laps.

To be honest, I didn't want to talk. All I wanted to do was think. Think how am I going to make it up to Maya. How to try and make her forget what she has been through? Maybe I could buy her $1000-dollar worth of toys and ice cream? Not enough. Take her to Disneyland? Nope.

I know it, I know what I have to do but me, being selfish again I can't. I should give her the gift of fatherhood. I should give her a father who would love her and care for her but I am too much of a coward to do that.

No! Enough is enough! This was the last straw and I am tried of being selfish and a coward and worst of being a liar! I am telling everyone the truth, today.

Chapter 40

Does the clock always tic this loud, or is it me losing my mind? Is it okay that I am feeling so hot in the middle of December? Is this usual that I feel my lungs aren't giving me enough amount of oxygen that I believe I need?

No, this can't be. It's all in my head; I am sure of it.

I close my eyes for a precious moment and take deep breath then I let it out slowly. I repeated this exercise for about 3 times then I started to feel better.

Everyone was already in the living room as I asked them. They were waiting for me to tell them what 'big news' I had. If only doing the good thing was as easy as it sounded.

The most thing I am terrified to figure out is how Zayn and Maya will react to this. Okay, well maybe Maya won't really understand now but one day she'll grow and ask me how doesn't she remember anything about her father at the age of 4.

Maybe I should tell Zayn in private first?

"C'mon Mariam! We don't have all day long!" Louis shouted.

Well there is no time and I gotta do it now. No changing my mind and no turning back.

I walk into the living room. God! Everyone is watching very movement and it's killing me.

I release one more deep breath before talking. "There is something which I have been keeping from all of you for a long time and couldn't quite bring myself to tell anyone but two people. It's really taking a huge part of me to tell you this now."

"Please go ahead and do so because you are making me so anxious." Niall mutters.

"I never got a chance to talk about Maya's father. I don't do that a lot or at all to be honest. All I told you was that he isn't Justin but I never told you who he really was." My breathing was barely able to keep it's pace.

"If you ever thought of it, Maya is 4 years old, which means I had her almost 5 years ago. In high school." I swallowed the lump in my throat, trying my best not to look at Zayn. Then suddenly, he stands up. "She's mine, isn't she?" I have never seen Zayn cry my whole life except maybe once or twice but not much tears ever left his eyes but today is the first time in my whole life Zayn's eyes were so shinny more than they are supposed to be yet not single tear lets go of his eye.

"Zayn." I call out his name taking a step closer but he placed his hand in between us, lightly pushing me away. "I asked you a question, please answer me." He isn't even looking at me.

"Zayn, please listen to me. I was 18 and I didn't know what to-" He cut me off.

"There you go again with the excuses! Could you stop for a moment and fucking take responsibility for your fucking mistakes for once!" Zayn shouted with so much anger.

"Zayn, I am taking all responsibility for this and this is why I am telling you this now. Please just bare in mind that I was a helpless 18-year-old and the only fucking time I tried to tell someone about my pregnancy, they tried to hit me then died, the only thing my father will remember about me is how I let him down and how much of a disappointment I am." Tears where in no place to be held back. They ran down my cheek like it was a race track.

"Look Zayn, I am not saying I did the right thing but I was scared you wouldn't want to be a part of the baby's life."

"So you fucking made that choice yourself?" He says mockingly. "I was a teenager too by the way; 19 isn't that old nor wise but I was willing to take that chance. I was willing to be a father. I would have wanted to help but you didn't ask for my consent. You just ran away from your problems like you always do." He headed towards the door.

Gathering the last breathe in me before I break down, "I am not asking for forgiveness or sympathy. I told you this because I was sick and tired of keeping secrets and because life doesn't promise any tomorrows, only todays. All I'm asking is to take your time and think it through and please don't blame Maya for my mistakes. She need a father."

"Now you see that." Zayn huffs, slamming the door behind him.

I felt like my heart just shattered. Despite all the pain in body, my heart hurt most. I didn't even think twice before running to my room and cry my heart out, just like a little girl that got her heart broken by her middle school crush.

I wasn't crying about Zayn but about the situation itself was awful and not knowing how will he act to Maya but even worse, how will I tell her?

This is too much. My life was okay just a couple of months ago, we had some financial problems but nothing some extra work hours couldn't fix but now I don't even know what's functioning in my life.

A soft knocking on my door echoed through my room. "Please leave me alone." My tears still going on. I got up stared at myself in the mirror. My eyes are so red and puffy, nose is red and swollen and my whole face was burning filled with red spots. "Zayn probably can't hate me more than I already do anyway." I whisper to my mirror-self.

My door opened and Harry stepped in. He looked sad, he was probably disappointed in me, I mean who wouldn't?

"Mariam," He starts off. "What you did was terribly wrong and I can't believe you would do such thing." He trails off.

Yep, I knew he hated me too.

"But I don't hate you and I never will. I am your only brother and we don't have anyone but each other now. I want you to know that you did the right thing today and I am pretty sure that must have been really hard for and I really appreciate it but for Zayn to forgive you, you'll have to give him a lot of time and a reason not give up on you."

"He loves you. He really does. You should have seen him when you were kidnapped, he stayed up all night long, he went to each police station everyday just to get one single piece of information about you,

and when we found Maya, she would cry a lot and do noting but ask for you. He stayed up with her and sang her to sleep. He made sure she ate everyday. He took her preschool everyday. He was like a father to her without even knowing it. He loves both of you too much to let you go and I promise he'll come around just give him some time and space."

I hugged Harry so tight I think he stopped breathing for a second. "Thank you, Harry. Thank you so much."

Hours pass and the clock tic and toc all time long. I have never been so nervous. I don't even know why I am so anxious anymore, there is much shit going on my head, everything scares me. I might stop crying for a moment or so but then when no one is talking and nothing is keeping the void in my mind occupied, my brain tries to entertain me with these thrilling memories. My eyes were starting to tear up again when the front door opened and Zayn walked in.

He looked calmer than before. I wipe away my tears before anyone can see but it's not like he noticed my presence anyway. I get up and walk over to him slowly. He was headed upstairs, "Zayn.." I call quietly. He turned around. I couldn't really make out his face expression, but it was a mix of hatred, sadness and anger, a lot of it. I could smell some alcohol on him. He raised his eyebrow at me, motioning for me to speak. "I won't even apologize because I know that there are no enough amount of 'sorry's that could turn back time. I am willing to give you all the time and space you need. I will wait for you even for a thousand years." I managed to say this without breaking down into tears but I took 2 or 3 breathing breaks in between.

"And before you say anything, I don't just care about Maya but I love you Zayn. I love you so much that I can't live without you." He still trying get a hold of what I am saying. He doesn't seem drunk but he might be a little tipsy. "Did you rehearse this speech before I walked in?" He mimicked.

"Zayn, please. I'll give you all the time you want with Maya to try and make up for all of this." I say hopelessly.

"Oh! You'll give some time extra time with Maya. That's really generous of you. How can I ever repay you?" He laughs.

He stopped for a moment and then his grin washed away and anger reappeared. "I am going to take custody of Maya. 'You' can come visit her." He empathized on the 'you'.

"Zayn Please!" I feel like my breathes are too shallow. My whole fucking world is falling down. "Don't take her away from me. I don't have anything but her. Please Zayn as your friend do not take her away from me." I plead him.

"I am doing what's better for her!" He shouts. "Do you have money? Can you put a roof over her head? Fucking hell you can't even pick her up from preschool."

I just stood there feeling each word he says like a knife being stabbed in my back. Of all people I never thought I'd hear these words come out of Zayn's mouth.

Where is the Zayn that was worried sick about me? Where is the one I fell in love with?

My hands were shaking so bad but I wanted to hide it, "Don't blame Maya for what I did! She doesn't have to grow up without her mother. Please Zayn, for the sake our friendship."

"As a friendly advice, you should get a really good lawyer but between you and me, it's no use anyway." He walks to room's door, with me following but then the second before he enters he turns around to face me, he scans me for half a second.

"I can't fucking believe I didn't figure this out earlier. But you know what's really ironic? I really envied Maya's father because 'he' had such a beautiful daughter and you, of course but now that I know I am him, I'd rather trade you." I understand that he's hurt, he is saying this out of pain and I get it but as much as I know this, it still hurt just as if I don't.

"Zayn this is not the real you. You are caring and loving-"

"Turns out both of us don't really know each other that well." He slams his door.

I could feel my chest tighten and tears come back rushing to my eyes. I started walking to my room while I can barely see. I feel so light headed. Out of nowhere, Louis appears in front of me. I break down completely, I fall to my knees and cry and cry. Even though I am not looking at Louis, I could sense that he's next to me. I feel his hands slide behind me and he holds me while resting his chin on my head. "I fucked up, big time." I cry into his shirt. "It will be alright, I promise." He whispers into my hair.

Chapter 41

I couldn't sleep yesterday at all. I tried to sleep in all positions possible: on my back, right side, fetal position, left side then again on my back. Maya was sound asleep so that's another reason why didn't want to move too much. I turned one last time, and gazed at her beautiful face. "I love you so much and I really hope you know that. I am so sorry you have to pay the price of my mistakes, I am so sorry." I whisper in the lowest voice I can make.

I get up and walk to the bathroom. Of course, I am crying again. Apparently, that's all I ever do now. I bite my lower lip to stop any further tears planning to run down my cheeks. Pulling my weak body all the way downstairs was really tiring. I head over to the kitchen and guess who's there?

Zayn. Fucking great! Just great!

I walk in, not making a sound and he still hasn't raised his head from his phone. To be honest, I don't want him to. I don't have anything new to tell him. I don't have anything valuable to offer him and he has no reason to stop what he is doing.

The coffee smells so good. I used to always drink it with milk and two sugars but then Zayn told me to not add sugar because he didn't like it and time after time I forgot what sugar tasted like and I believed that all the sugar I needed was in his mouth which I get to explore with my own tongue but now everything feels tasteless. Now that I don't get to kiss his lips and taste his sugar, my coffee seems so dark, and bitter. Yeah bitter describes it better.

"If you're looking for the sugar it's in the cupboard." He nonchalantly says. His voice is so dull but at least he is acknowledging me.

I wasn't about to tell him that I didn't want this sugar. "Do you want some?" That was all that came out of my mouth. "Already had mine." He points to the empty cup next to him.

I nod even though I know he hadn't glanced at me even once since I entered. He seems to be too busy with what's going on behind his plastic screen.

I decided to drink it as it is; if I add so much sugar I might forget what his lips felt like and start to like this synthetic sugar again.

What's killing me most is that he is sitting right there! I mean I can go there and kiss him so hard that our lips go numb from all the impact and heat that will devour his lips.

As soon as I let my hair down and get a little taste of hope which turns out to be just the aftertaste of this unsweetened coffee. The moment I take my first step towards the counter, he jumps up. "All yours." He mutters running out of the kitchen.

Have I become so poisonous, that he can't bare the sight of me?

I sip the coffee, feeling nothing but bitterness each time. I bring the mug to my mouth. I have to be honest with you, it doesn't really taste that bad. It's only the memories it's dipped in, they are killing me.

I realized my phone was in my pocket so I grabbed it and started wandering endlessly through my Instagram feed. All these people so perfect and happy. Happy. I forgot what that word sounded like. I can't remember the last time was like genuinely happy, like so happy that nothing could have brought me down.

That would definitely be the day Maya was born.

I remember it so well.

Flashback

"Come on Mariam!" My aunt, Rachel screams. "Just hold on." She says holding my hand. I nodded weakly in response. I have been pushing for so long and Maya is almost out but it's so painful.

"Come on baby." Rachel holds me tighter. I grip really tight on her hand and push as hard as I can. Then I felt it, the baby was out! I didn't want to know if I was having a girl or boy. I wanted to keep it a surprise and my aunt respected that but she told me she wanted to know so she already does.

I was so weak at this very moment but I didn't want to close my eyes until I see my baby. "She is so beautiful!" My aunt yells. So it's a she. She's going to be a mini me! "Oh dear! I am so sorry. I didn't mean to spoil I-" She puts her hand on her mouth. "It's o-okay." I barely mumble.

After a few seconds the doctor brought her to my arms. She was so small. I don't why I was crying but I couldn't stop.

Do you know that feeling when you meet someone for the first time and you just know that you'll love them till the day you die? This was exactly how I felt right now.

"She looks just like you." My aunt was crying. I take a moment to soak in what she just said but she was wrong, so wrong. She was a lot like Zayn. I know it was too early to tell but I felt it deep in my bones. "Please-e don't-t c-cry." I place my arm over her. "What will you name her?"

"Maya." My mum wanted to name me Maya but dad didn't really like it and they decided to go with something uncommon and not American. I think my name is of Arabic origin. Maya means magic in Indian culture and she is my source of magic.

"Hello little Maya. I am the big old lady called mommy. I am going to care of you, feed you and teach you vulnerable lessons but most importantly I will be your best friend. I'll never leave your side." I cooed at her while she was still in my arms. "May I?" My aunt asks, motioning towards Maya's petit body. I smile and push Maya gently towards her.

She takes her from arms very carefully as if she is fragile. I love how tender she is with Maya. My aunt was the mother I never had. She taught me all the things I needed, and without her I would have never made it out alive.

"You'll make a wonderful mother, baby." She smiles at me. "Now rest a little."

Little did she know my eyes were already closing on their own.

Flashback

"MOMMY!" Maya screams running down the stairs. I looked over towards where her voice was coming from. I saw her running towards me. Then she jumps at my legs as soon she sees me. "I lwve you!" She mumbles.

I place my hands under her arms and pull on my lap. She looked so excited and filled with happiness. Maya's got this contagious kind of smile that when look at for too long, you wouldn't be able to resist it. In a matter of seconds I was smiling back. "I love you too, babygirl." I kiss her forehead. "Now let's go eat breakfast!"

"But I don't like bweakfast, mommy." She frowns. "I am not mommy. I am the Cookie Monster and I will eat you!!" I shout as I tickle her stomach. She giggles with all power she has. Her giggles are so addictive. She always scrunches her nose and closes her eyes shut when she laughs, just like Zayn does.

Zayn's POV:

After what happened I was devastated and I felt betrayed because I loved her so much! I would have died for her but right now I don't know how I feel towards her. She lied to me for all these years.

I can't say I hate her but I don't think I can trust her again and I am not letting her get away with lying to me just like that. "MOMMY!" I heard Maya scream. Did something happen to her? I rushed over to her voice.

I saw Maya running as fast as her little feet could take her to her mum. She hugged her legs. Then Mariam placed her on her laps. I couldn't quite make out what they were saying but I bet it was something funny because Maya was overflowing with laughter as Mariam was tickling her tummy.

God, she looked so vibrant when she was happy. I let out a breath. Why am I still thinking about her? They both looked so happy.

My mind can't help but wonder what if Mariam just told me that day the she was pregnant? We would have been a beautiful family right now, living in UK still. Maya might have had a baby brother or sister, mostly a brother. We might have been married even.

But this is all in my head and it's not going to happen ever.

No! No, I won't be weak, I will take custody of Maya. She is my daughter just like she is her's. I love Maya with all my heart and I would do anything to make her happy. "Mommy!" Maya screams only this time she wasn't so excited as before but there was horror lacing her voice this time.

I rushed to the kitchen and saw Mariam on the floor unconscious and Maya was crying her eyes out on the counter. "Zayn! Help mommy!!" She cries.

Chapter 42

I couldn't believe my eyes! "Zayn! Is mommy gonna be okay?" Maya was crying. "Yes, Princess. I promise you she will be. I kneeled down panicking. Think! Think! What do I do first? Call 911. I reached for my phone and started to tap the phone icon but my fingers were shaking.

"Ughhh! Damnit!" I scream. Maya begins to cry a little louder. "Don't worry Maya. I promise mommy will be okay." I try to calm her and myself. I let out a deep breath and type in the digits then press call. "Hello. This is 911. What's your emergency?"

"My-eh-wife is passed out in the kitchen and I don't know what do?"

Don't even ask, it was just the first word the popped into my head. "I am sending an ambulance to your place right now, sir." The lady at the other end of the line says.

"Check her breathing and pulse, Sir."

I did as she informed me and checked it. "She is barely breathing and her pulse is weak." I was panicking and I didn't want Maya to see this.

I grab Mariam in my lap and rock her. "You can't bail on Maya, okay!" I shout at her unconscious body. "She needs you! I need you." I mumbled the last part.

"Sir? Are you still there?" Shit! I forgot that I am still on the phone. "Y-Yes. Her breathing is getting weaker." I mumble. "The ambulance is on it's way, sir."

As I was analyzing Mariam's face I realized how badly she was sweating. This is definitely not good. "She is sweating a lot, like really really a lot." I notify the lady. "This is not good." She says in a concerned tone.

"Maya! I need you to go wake up the lads." I order and she nods. Maya pushes her little self off of the counter and runs out of the kitchen. "Just hold on." I whisper to Mariam.

*

'This is not happening. This is not happening. This in not happening.' I'll repeat this to myself a hundred times if I have to. Mariam is in the emergency room right now and I do really believe that this hospital needs a better ventilation system because I can't fucking breathe.

The lads are at home with Maya. I told them I don't feel comfortable having Maya see her mother like this. And I need to know that Mariam is fine then I'll ask the lads to bring Maya here.

I fall onto the plastic chair next to me and stare deeply at my lap. I kept bouncing my legs up and down. The wait is killing me. I stood up again. I blow out some excess air I find in my lungs. "What's taking them so long?" I maffle to my worried persona, in hope that would calm me a little.

After what seemed like decades, the doctor appeared. He looked in his late forties. He had blond hair and hazel brown eyes.

I rush over to his direction. "Hello-Mr Malik?" He says trying to make sure he got the name right. "Yes, that me."

"I am Dr.Willson but please call me Kevin." He extends his hand for me to shake and I do so.

"And I believe my patient's name is Mariam Malik, as in your wife is that right?" I nod.

He lets out a breath the starts speaking. "Sir, have you been having any problems with your wife?"

"What do you mean?" I take that question offensively. "Like have you been having any usual husband and wife fights? Has she been having any problems at work? With the kids? If you have any?"

"No-I don't think so." I wasn't really sure what he meant. "Is it no or you don't think so, sir?" He is really starting to get on my nerves.

"I am not really sure but can you tell me what's wrong with my wife?" I clench my jaw in order to release stress. "Well, sir your wife is dealing with a lot of stress that it harmed her physically."

'I-I did this, didn't I?'

"We made a whole body check up and we found nothing serious but yet she was showing a lot of stress symptoms such as sweating, high blood pressure, heart palpitations and a few others."

I can't speak. I genuinely feel like my tongue is tied. No words are coming out. "So apparently, her high blood pressure caused the dizziness and this caused her to black out." He informs me. "I know you might think stress isn't that much of a problem but it is. You said that your wife fell unconscious in kitchen and thank god nothing serious happened this time but what if she hit her head on kitchen counter or a table, or even left the stove on." I nod. What he didn't know was that I was too shocked to form representable words.

"I understand that really well." He nods one last time before starting to walk away but then he stops mid way. "And sir, one last question."

"Is your wife on any kind of medication?" What kind of question is that? Does he suspect Mariam is doing drugs?

"Not that I know of."

"Well via a blood test we made, we found out that your wife might have been taking a little doze of heroine." He must be fucking kidding.

"I am pretty sure I must report this to the police." My eyes widen at his statement. "But since you seem like a nice man I can make you an offer. You could ask your wife why was she doing it and ask her for her dealer and then we'll report him to the police instead of her." He smirks. "My wife isn't on anything! It's not my problem that you can't do your fucking job!" This was the last straw so I just exploded.

"I am really sorry, sir but the police will believe the one who has the actual blood test and not the guy who doesn't even know if his wife is dealing with stress." My blood was boiling and I was retaining myself from killing him so bad.

"So shall I make that call now or wait?" He says again in his calm mother fucking voice. "Wait. I'll take your stupid offer." I bite on my teeth so hard I think they will break.

"Dr.Willson! She is awake!" A nurse rushes in. I give him a dirty look then enter her room. She was lying so helplessly on her white hospital bed. 'I did this to her' This thought hit me as soon as I saw her. She seemed surprised by my presence.

Mariam's POV:

I was feeling so lightheaded. I saw a male's silhouette make his was into the room. After I gained some consciousness I made out he was Zayn! What is he doing here?

"Z-Zayn?" I call, not believing my eyes. "I am so sorry." He mumbles moving closer to me. "I did this to you." He cries. He was genuinely crying. "I never meant to hurt you. Mariam, I love you so much. I tried to hate you and I tried to hurt your feelings but I ended up getting hurt even more." He was crying his eyes out. I was shocked! "Z-Zayn, I am fine now." I try to calm him down.

"No, you're not and I did this. Mariam after I fell in love with you I swore myself I would never hurt you again but I broke my own promise and I hurt you. I was blinded by my stupidity and selfishness. I hated that you had Maya and she loved you so much and I envied that." I have never seen Zayn so honest before.

"You should see the way she looks at you, the way she laughs when you touch her. I am so sorry I ever tried to come in between you." He was full on sobbing. "Zayn, it's okay, I swear."

"Stop saying it is because it's not!" He shouts. "You could have hit your head! You could have died today because of me!" He screams.

I don't answer anymore. I now know that my replies are meaningless. They won't ever give him the comfort he needs. Zayn falls to his knees. "I am the source of misery in your life. And I wanted to take Maya from you-"

"But you didn't! You stopped before things got out of hand! Now, pull yourself together and come fucking kiss me or I will make you come here myself!" I shout. He looked at me with a teary smile that made me cry.

"I hate you; you're making me cry, Malik." He comes closer and kisses me. "I love you too." He mumbles in between our kissing. Then he stops, "Mariam." Zayn calls which really freaks me out.

"Something wrong?" I tilt my head a little. "Did-did you do anything illegal?" I can't believe the words coming out his mouth. "Like what?"

"Did you take unauthorized drugs?"

Chapter 43

"What kind of question is that? Why would I ever do that?" I ask him. "The doctors found some heroine in your blood through a blood test. I am so worried; they want to use it against you." He explains. "B-But I never took such thing-" Then it hit me hard. "But I know who might have gave it to me." Zayn looks at me.

"Justin drugged me." Tears rush to my eye as soon as I start having flash-backs but Zayn didn't notice. "That son of a bitch." Zayn yells. "If I get my hands on him, I won't let go till he's fucking dead." Zayn spats with venom lacing his voice. But Zayn's words didn't make me feel better, they made me cry even harder. My lips were trembling and eyes were turning red.

"Mariam, please don't cry." Zayn hugs me. "You really need to think about reporting Justin. He kidnapped you, he abused you physically and he drugged you. I'll get you the best lawyer I know and will do everything we can to place that bitch where he belongs; behind bars."

I know this is the right thing to do but I am so scared. I'll have to confess all the things he did to me in front a judge, an attorney, the jury and even him. He'll be inches away from me. He'll staring at me the whole time I try to form words, just to scare me.

"It's going to be so hard." My breaths were shallow by now. "Mariam," Zayn looks me straight in my eyes. "But you'll get what you deserve, you'll do whatever you want without feeling scared to go out. You think I haven't noticed all bruises and cuts on your body? This is not fair!"

"This guy who harmed the woman I love and my daughter in all ways possible, gets to have his happily ever after? If you won't do it for yourself, do it for Maya." As soon as he said Maya's name I realized that this not my fight only to give up but I really do owe Maya her right even if I want to give up mine.

I nodded in response but Zayn stopped me mid way, crashing his lips on mine. His kiss gave me comfort, his whole presence did. "Zayn?" I call.

Zayn's POV:

"Yes?" I answer her. "I didn't tell you about Maya because I was terribly and utterly sacred. I can't lie I thought maybe you'd get angry-" She is looking at her hands. "I-I really wanted to.." She was crying. God! Seeing her cry kills me. "After telling my father and what happened...I-I just couldn't." She pauses for a moment to catch her breath.

"I have been abused by every male figure in my life and I didn't believe that what we had was going to actually last."

"Mariam," I cut her. "Please let me finish-" Her breaths were short and fast. Tears ran down her red soft cheeks. "I thought I was gonna move on from you someday and so will you. I thought we'd grow out of it." She bits her lips. "But I never fell out of love with you. I never loved Justin but he was a good distraction until he turned abusive." I was analyzing each moment and her body language gave off a vastly sad vibe.

I felt like all the air was knocked out of me. I want to take it all back. I want to take every single time I hurt her back then in highschool. Why did I ever lay my hand on her? How could I let myself go this far?! If only I knew what she was going through! I would have fucking took every single beating for her.

I couldn't hold back my tears, I tried to I swear. "Mariam, I am the luckiest man in the whole world because I have such a strong woman in my life. You faced this horrible universe's torture with love and a warm smile. You were too pure to be here." She was now looking at me with her teary eyes as wide as they can be.

"I am so sorry. I have been so selfish in the way that I reacted and I have been taking a lot of things for granted at the very top of that list was you." I hold her hand.

"You don't understand how beautiful you are inside out. Mariam, after all this hate you got from the world, yet you raised our child with all the love you had." I realized I never used 'our child' before but it sounds so right.

I wouldn't have imagined it any other way. Me, her and our little princess, that must be what heaven looks like. "I really didn't want to say this but you have been abusing yourself also. You didn't give yourself any credit for how hard you have been holding on. A lot of people tried to bring you down, including me but I realized I was so wrong and I have been living in regret ever since, but you didn't stop hurting yourself!" I stare deeply in her eyes.

"Give yourself some credit cause you deserve it. Hell, a lot of it." I didn't believe what happened next she hugged me. I was caught off guard but then I held her so tight. "You know what's so perfect about you?"

Before she could even open her mouth I answered my own question. "It's that even when the world beat you down you got back up again but not seeking revenge, only seeking love and kindness. I have never seen a person so kind-hearted like that before." I finish off.

She just holds on tighter to my torso. "Zayn," She calls. "Huh?" I answer. "You are the reason I made it out of this hell. If it weren't for Maya back then I am pretty sure I would have committed suicide or something and if it weren't for you right now, I wouldn't have never made it out alive." Her look is so innocent.

How can she look like an angel?

"I promise you, Mariam, I'll be by your side each step of the way." I kiss her forehead.

*

Mariam was resting for a little bit, the nurse gave her some sedatives. Poor her because of me, she wasn't able to sleep at all. I called the lads and they were on their way with Maya.

This must be what people warn you about in love, how you feel like you'll do anything for this person you love very deeply, how you feel like you can take on the world when you're together. This feeling is addictive, and here lies the problem, this isn't a once in a lifetime kinda thing.

This feeling comes along with the person you love, and the more time you spend next with them the more you get that feeling and the more you feel like you need it and crave it even more.

I am an addict. I lie here guilty, as I am addicted to her, her love, her voice, her aura. I love being even around her. I didn't want to confess it but I am wrapped around her little finger.

She's literally perfection and I hate it so much when she sees herself anything less than that! She faced so much pain in her life that even I didn't go through. Too much abuse, too much pain, too much hate and on the top that she was all alone but yet she never complained.

I hate how I miss-judged her, miss-treated her. And I shall hate the young me for ever thinking it was okay to lay a finger on her. I steal a look at her while she sleeping peacefully for the first time in so long.

I walk over to her bed and hold her hand. "I let you down and you being your forgiving-self, you gave me another chance without even thinking twice about it."

"If only-I can turn back time, I'd give you a reason to trust me, to have faith in me and tell me, not only about the pregnancy but everything!"

"Your abusive father, how much you missed your mother?, your dreams, your thoughts, anything. I would have been your shoulder that you can cry on when you feel a little sad, lean on when you need someone by your side. I would have been there if only I realized that earlier." A tear let hold of my eye and made it's way down my cheek.

"So here I am, again apologizing, and I'll keep doing it till the day I die because of how I let you down." I felt my chest actually hurting me.

Is this the guilt? Is this the regret I'll have to carry till I meet my creator?

"Hey mate!" I heard someone scream but before I could even turn around a little brown-haired creature was glued to my legs. "I missed you." She mumbled. All the air got knocked out of me after hearing those words.

I bend over and pick Maya up. "Zayn?" She calls, pushing her beautiful hair out of her face. "Is mommy okay? Can we go home now?" She looks at me with her enchanting big brown eyes. "Mommy is fine but she is resting for a little bit because she didn't sleep well." She nodded cautiously.

"Everything alright, mate?" Harry motions over to me. "Yeah, yeah. Can you take Maya for a second?"

He extended his arms for Maya to jump in and she does so. "Excuse me-"
I run to the restroom. I take a few breath and organize their in and outs
rhythm.

I grasp onto the sink so hard then slowly look up at the mirror. I made a
mistake, a huge one but I will fix it.

Chapter 44

- -

Mariam's POV:

"Did he hurt you physically?" Zayn's attorney asked me. I nodded. "Could you be a little more specific?" He asked. "He would hit me if we disagreed about something or if I didn't obey him." I barely breathe out. "Most of the usual beatings would be a mixture of punches and kicks but if he was really angry, choking would definitely be involved."

"Did he abuse you sexually?" The air got knocked out of my lungs. "N-no." I more like scream.

I felt Zayn's hand on mine. He held my hand in his so gently. He gave me a reassuring smile.

Our lawyer grabbed his notebook and files. "I think this is enough for today. Thank you for your time. Now if you'll excuse me."

Zayn's Pov:

"Did he abuse you sexually? As soon as this question left Kane's lips, Mariam's body tensed up and I could feel her panic. She was at a loss of words. "N-no." She kind of shouts.

I go over and hold her hand tightly yet with delicacy. She looked at me and I smiled at her and she calmed a little.

I motioned to Kane that this was enough for now so he started to collect his things. "I think this is enough for today. Thank you for your time. Now if you'll excuse me." I got up and shook hands. "Thank you." I mouthed to him and he nodded then walked out.

I closed the door then walked to Mariam. She was still silent when I was near her. When I was close enough she looked at me.

Her eyes were a little bit glassier than usual. She jumped in my arms. I didn't need to ask her, I knew the answer, not the one she blurted out to skip the question but the genuine one.

"He'll pay for this, all of it." I rest my chin on her head.

Mariam's pov:

I didn't want to be asked any questions, I just wanted someone to hold me.

He hurt me in so many ways, so so many ways and I kept my mouth shut.

Flashback

"Get in!" Justin screamed, pushing me inside. "I told you I wasn't flirting with your stupid friend! He was the one hitting on me." I shouted at him.

I didn't prepare for what I was going to happen next. He slapped me with so much force that I backed away.

"D-don't touch me. Don't-t fucking-g lay a finger on me-e." I catch my breath. He lunched himself forward and grabbed my throat, pinning my limp body to the wall behind me.

"You don't get to shout orders here." He roars. "Understand?!" His grip tightens. "I-I can't-t breathe-e." My eyes start to tear up. "Good." He whispered in my ear.

Nothing but fear was running through my veins. When he realizes I am weak enough, he lets go of my neck. I collapse hopelessly to the floor, panting and yearning for a breath. I trace the newly formed bruise on my neck.

"You are an asshole!" I cry. He stood there in his Tom Ford tuxedo, watching my every move.

My heart hurts, it actually hurts. "And you're just a pathetic slut." His index finger lifted my chin to face him. "Maybe if you showed me some attention then your sadistic friends wouldn't hit on me."

His clam expression changed into a furious one. "You want attention?" He clenched his jaw. Justin yanked a fistful of my hair and threw me on the couch.

In a blur, he was on the top of me. He pinned my arms above me with one hand while the other was pulling up my Versace dress. "I'll fucking give you attention."

His hands aimed for my panties, pulling them down. "N-no, please. Please Justin! You can't do this." I cry heavily. He unbuckles his belt and throws it across the room then pushes his pants and boxers. "Oh but babe, I can."

Then he... he.. did what he did to me. He pushed the breath out my lungs. He ruined me.

Now, my brain will forever hold this agonizing feeling and memory.

When he was done he pulled his boxers and pants but before he walked away, "You know what, you're actually right. You definitely deserve more attention." He picks up his belt and walks away.

I push my dress over me to cover what's left of me untouched. I was shaking, my legs were shaking so hard they hurt. My whole body hurts me. I felt disgusted by my own body. I break down into tears.

I wanted to scream so loud but my voice betrayed me, my lungs did too and my whole body did.

I can't breathe! I can't breathe! I can't breathe!

Flashback

I told Zayn every little detail. I felt Zayn's tension just by touching him. "I will fucking kill him." Zayn clenched his jaw. "I never told anyone, not even my aunt-" I was panting again.

He kissed my forehead and hugged me. "I am so sorry you had to face this alone." His warm embrace was so soothing and relaxing. "Zayn, please stop apologizing. You didn't do anything." I tell him. "I did Mariam, I did. It's just what I did wasn't so obvious. I pushed you away and I didn't make you believe you could trust me. If I gave you a good reason to stay, you would have been still at UK."

"No, Zayn. I would have still gone to USA because my aunt lives here or else I would have been thrown in an orphanage." I stare deeply in his eyes. "This. Is. Not. Your. Fault." I repeat. "Mariam, I love you." His lips hold a tight grip on mine.

"You should know that if I catch that bitch before the police does, then he's a dead bitch." Zayn says and it makes me crack a teary smile.